A
_____
CANDLELIGHT REGENCY SPECIAL

CANDLELIGHT ROMANCES

BRIDE OF CHANCE

LUCY PHILLIPS STEWART

A CANDLELIGHT REGENCY SPECIAL

Published by
Dell Publishing Co., Inc.
1 Dag Hammarskjold Plaza
New York, New York 10017

Dell ® TM 681510, Dell Publishing Co., Inc.

ISBN: 0-440-10810-1

Printed in the United States of America
First printing—October 1978

BRIDE OF CHANCE

CHAPTER I

Attired in blue and silver, and with diamonds on his fingers and in the lace at his throat, John George Alastair, Duke of Acton, lounged back in his chair, one hand still grasping a deck of cards, a look of aloof disdain upon his face. The glow of candles in the chandelier above his head shot points of light from the jewels he wore and made his eyes glitter queerly. No one observing the play could fail to realize that his Grace had imbibed quite deeply. Only those among the company more intimately acquainted with his lordship could recognize and so secretly applaud the seeming air of unconcern with which his hard gaze lingered for a moment on the face of his opponent. Lord Orling, himself in a state of inebriety fast approaching oblivion, nevertheless retained a sufficient hold on reality to find himself unable to meet those strangely piercing eyes. For his mind, fuzzy though it was with drink, retained one thought: he had wagered his stepdaughter in a game with Acton, and lost.

His Grace shook back Dresden ruffles from his hand, smiled with sardonic humour upon his friends, and made his way with quite wonderful balance out of the club. Declining the porter's offer to whistle up a chair, he set off aimlessly in the direction of St. James's Square, his head clearing a little as he strolled along in the cool night air. He felt remote, detached from his surroundings, and not a little sorry for himself as he reflected bitterly on his curious fate. By now in full possession of his heretofore somewhat befuddled faculties, he had not the least difficulty in ascertaining to a nicety what the future held in store. At the depressing picture thus called up, an unmistakable shudder ran through his frame. Never in his wildest imaginings had he expected to propose marriage to a lady he had never seen. For he must marry the girl. To do less would bring dishonour upon the name he bore. Arriving finally before his own door, he sighed and, slowly mounting the front steps, passed within.

At precisely eleven of the clock on the following morning he stepped down from his carriage drawn up before Orling House, directed his coachman to wait for him, and strolled in leisurely fashion up the steps and through the door. Lord Orling having been denied, he inquired for his lordship's stepdaughter, his face showing little emotion upon being informed that her ladyship was indeed at home. Ushered by a reluctant footman into the small salon on the ground floor, he crossed with long strides to take up a stance before the fire, his coat of superfine cloth and biscuit-coloured pantaloons showing not one crease in moulding broad shoulders and muscular thighs. He bore himself with easy arrogance, and if any flaw could be discovered in his appearance it lay in his air of cynical boredom and in the weary disillusion in his eyes. Looking not in the least like a gentleman living in happy anticipation of his betrothal, he declined all offers of refreshment and turned his back to the room, to stare down into the fire.

Jessica, meanwhile, paused at the top of the long staircase, her hands clenched at her sides, and blinked back the tears. She did not look at the butler preceding her down the flight, nor at any of the footmen on duty in the hall below. No one of them so much as glanced at her, but kept their eyes carefully averted, their commiseration causing her to wince a little. For the morning caller was the gentleman who had, last evening, won her in a game of cards. There could be no doubt. Her drunken stepfather had staked her person, and lost.

As she slowly descended the stairs, she reflected, not for the first time that morning, on the note she had earlier received on the crested stationery of the Duke of Acton begging permission to call—the usual courteous missile. His signature had failed to bring up any vision of his countenance, for she had never, to her knowledge, met him. But she had heard much of him, none of it to the good. It was not enough to say that he was the bearer of an old and respected title, nor did it much signify that he possessed great wealth. For he had, from all accounts, long devoted himself to an unceasing pursuit of all the more reprehensible forms of scandalous behaviour.

Arriving at the doorway of the small salon, she stood quietly observing him for a moment before making her presence known to him. He did not appear so very villainous; hopefully the more lurid tales of him would turn out to be mostly fabrication. "You wished to see me, your Grace?" she managed with admirable calm.

He turned at the sound of her voice, his wary expression giving way to one of mingled surprise and relief. A quick impression of dusky curls cascading to her nape where they were caught back told him it would fall to her waist when loosed. He was also aware of a milk-white skin and large, grey eyes. Had it occurred to him that she felt inclined to despise her beauty, he would have disapproved. He preferred brunettes, thinking blond hair insipid, and, being tall himself, favoured ladies rather above the average height. To her chagrin, he raised his quizzing glass and appraised her more precisely. "Good Lord!" he said. "Surely you aren't Jessica Cooke!"

It was so unexpected that she paused in moving forward. "Certainly I am," she replied with chilling hauteur. "Why should you doubt it?"

"Because you're by far too beautiful. I didn't come here expecting to find such a remarkably handsome woman."

Self-consequence, dissimilation, even indifference she could have pardoned. But this approach was beyond everything. She drew herself up to the fullest extent of her height, her wrath directed toward the creature before her. From the moment she first learned of the wager she had known that she despised him. Now that she had opportunity for the dubious pleasure of his acquaintance, she found that she disliked him no less. "Let me assure you, sir," she said frigidly, "your opinion is not of the least consequence to me."

It was now his turn to look disconcerted. She observed, with satisfaction, the flush creeping into his cheeks. "I didn't mean to bring you to daggers-drawn," he said finally.

"No doubt I should be grateful for that. I am not

accustomed so far as I can recall to the sort of incivility which you employ."

His penetrating gaze searched her face before he said, "I will endeavour to improve my conduct, though you must surely know I hadn't meant to put you out of temper. Will it relieve your mind to know I won't run rough-shod over you? I realize this interview is difficult, and I plan to make it as painless as possible."

"I am obliged to you for that," she replied with ironic gratitude. "Perhaps you will accommodate me further by forcibly putting the entire affair out of your thoughts. That, I might add, will relieve my own mind."

"You have had audience with your stepfather, I see, so you are aware of the position in which we find ourselves. You have been made the victim of our vicious actions, for which I apologize. Nothing, let me tell you, was further from my intention or, in truth, my wish. I mean now to do all within my power to scotch any scandal before it arises."

Her annoyance, and indeed her mortification, found expression in abrupt speech. "Be pleased not to concern yourself, your Grace. I plan to go to Nanny."

His eyes regarded her amicably. "I am afraid I cannot permit that," came his maddening reply.

To her horror, tears stung her eyelids. "You are mistaken, your Grace," she began in a voice that trembled slightly. She firmed it. "You are in no position to order my affairs. To own the truth, my lord, I had no notion of becoming the recipient of your missile, or of receiving a visit from you. I had not, after all, the very doubtful pleasure of your acquaintance."

She had intended this speech to quell further utterances from his tongue. To her chagrin he did not take instant umbrage. Instead of doing anything of the kind, he laughed. "That's set me down proper, hasn't it?" he said appreciatively.

"I devoutly hope so. I am not sufficiently well acquainted with you to know the degree of provocation you are able to withstand, but I should think it not excessive."

Amusement quivered in his eyes as he said, "What a refreshing creature you are, Lady Cooke. You have sustained a shock that should have sent you into the throes of extreme agitation, but instead you only rip up at me."

"Would you prefer I indulge in a fit of the vapors?"

"Certainly not. If there is one thing I cannot abide, it's the sight of any female turning herself into a watering pot."

She was obliged to smile, and to say, with innate honesty, "Well, and I cannot blame you for that. Neither can I."

"I would hazard a guess," he said mischievously, "that we might deal very well together if we try."

She was sorry to have unbent, even for a moment, and said, "Do not let us be standing about talking of it. I cannot think why we are."

"We are because you haven't invited me to sit. I'm not such a ramshackle fellow as to do so without your permission."

An uncomfortable echo of her words to him flashed through her mind, bringing a flush into her cheeks. "I'm afraid it is I who have been uncivil," she admitted, crossing to a chair. "Pray be seated, your Grace."

"Thank you," he murmured politely, controlling an errant tendency of his lips to twitch as he took a chair opposite hers. "And now, Lady Cooke, I have something to say, and I don't quite know how to go about it."

"That is nonsense. It seems a perfectly natural thing for you to proceed with the utmost disregard for my sensibilities."

"Good God, what will you say next!" he exclaimed, exasperated. "I have no doubt you would like to fob me off, but you have no choice in the matter. Will you kindly listen?"

"Oh for goodness sake. You needn't look daggers at me. Well, go ahead—if you must."

The sophisticated Duke of Acton was exhibiting signs of strain, unusual for him. Setting his jaw, he said through his teeth, "Will you do me the very great honour of becoming my wife?"

She regarded him with kindling eyes. "Certainly not!" she said.

He glared at her, a flush coming into his face. "You must realize we cannot remain unmarried after the deplorable events of last evening. Your good name would be irretrievably smirched. I cannot permit you to pay such a price for actions of which you are completely innocent."

"You should have thought of that last evening before you gambled for me with my stepfather," she shot back at him in biting accents. "However, that is neither here nor there. I shall join Nanny until I can make more suitable arrangements for my future. May I suggest that you concern yourself no further with my welfare."

He met the wrath in her eyes, and suddenly laughed. "Has anyone ever got the better of your tongue?" he asked, and waited expectantly.

He was not disappointed. "No," she said composedly.

"But then the gentlemen of my previous acquaintance have never exhibited a want of proper conduct."

"You must have found them dead bores."

She could not help smiling at that. "But eligible, sir," she said.

"The reason, I don't doubt, for your having remained unmarried. No, don't scowl at me, for it won't do, you know. You must have sustained innumerable suitors for your hand. Unless the gentlemen of your previous acquaintance have distinguished the propriety of their manners by a corresponding inability to find their tongues?"

"If you possessed one ounce of—of gentlemanly address, you would not be so abominable," she told him roundly. But her lips were exhibiting an inclination to smile and he could not miss the gleam in her eye.

"But just think of the pleasure, Lady Cooke, in comparing my lack of proper deportment with your own exemplary behaviour," he said gravely.

She noted the slight shake of his shoulders, and chuckled with him. "If you weren't such a rake-hell, my lord—"

His eyes alive with amusement, he said reprovingly, "Surely, ma'am, that is an expression unsuitable to the tongue of a delicately nurtured female?"

"Possibly it is, your Grace. But I shouldn't think you have been much in contact with ladies of quality."

"Are you quite certain we have not met?" he asked, the smile on his lips widening to a grin. "We must have for you to own such a masterly reading of my character."

"How can you be so detestable?" she returned, laughing in spite of herself. "Do, pray, stop trying to bring me around your finger. For it won't answer the purpose."

"Having been reared, alas, with no idea—unlike yourself—of how to be agreeable, I perfectly understand your prejudice against being saddled with me as a husband."

"While I, having been reared—unlike yourself—to respect common decency, perfectly understand that you should not be forced to marry me."

"I am not being forced to marry you. I prefer to do so." He added, with an impish grin, "I find myself becoming more reconciled to the notion by the minute."

"You astonish me, sir. I can't imagine why."

"It is my thought that the announcement of our betrothal must be sent to the papers this afternoon for inclusion in tomorrow's editions. We will determine the actual nuptial date when we have had time to make more specific plans. Our wedding will, of course, be the social event of the season. I trust this meets with your approval?"

"You must be out of your mind!"

"It is my intent to remove you from Orling House this afternoon," he continued imperturbably. "You cannot proceed directly to Acton House, as you no doubt realize. I plan to install you with my grandmother until our marriage."

"The Dowager Duchess!"

"Do not be frightened, Lady Cooke. She's really an old dear. You will deal well together, and with Grandmama your sponsor no tongue would dare to wag."

"Oh, no," she agreed with irony. "It would be quite unthinkable for anyone to do so—even if your grandmother were willing to embrace your preposterous scheme, which I very much doubt."

"Do you indeed? Then let me inform you that I have already made the necessary arrangements."

"What more can I say, your Grace, other than that it is a pity you have expended your energies needlessly."

"I haven't done any such thing. I perfectly understand how awkward the situation is for you, but if I must bullock you into marrying me, be assured I am prepared to do so."

"You are talking arrant nonsense. I have made it abundantly clear—"

"Is it your wish to remain under your stepfather's roof, Lady Cooke? Other than marriage with me, what other option is open to you? It is the worst folly to think you will be able to reside with your former Nanny. Unless I am very much mistaken, that good woman will be in no financial position to allow you to do so. It would be the height of impropriety to impose so outrageously on her meager living."

Casting a fulminating glance at him, she said crossly, "You've made a rare mess of my life, haven't you? Perhaps you will tell me why my situation should be any more insupportable with my stepfather than it would be with you?"

"Because I will not drive you to the point of desperation, as he assuredly would. Though I did not properly consider the natural consequences of the wager when I accepted it, it was your stepfather who staked your person in a game of cards, remember."

"My days used to be uneventful, but that, thanks to you, is a thing of the past. Well, you may be irredeemably toplofty, your Grace, but I will inform you that I have a mind of my own."

"Yes, I am aware of that," he returned affably. "And don't try to stir the coals, or I might be nudged into banking the fires. Marriage to me won't damage your nerves past mending."

"I don't recollect whether I have told you that you are abominable—"

"You have," he interjected, grinning. "You leave me no doubt that I have become a positive antidote."

"Oh, no," she gasped, somewhere between laughter and tears. "You're an ogre. I'm the antidote."

"You cannot have seen yourself in your looking glass. You will make a beautiful Duchess."

"Your Grace, are you quite certain you wish to marry me? I cannot think that society will ostracize you if you don't."

"If you but knew the excessively crucifying things society has said about me without ostracizing me, you would know not to employ that ruse."

She gave a choke of throaty laughter. "What an odiously wretched setback marriage will pose to your career," she gurbled irrepressibly.

The next instant he was before her, his tall, immaculate form seeming to blot out the room as he took her hands in his. "You are mistaken in that," he murmured half to himself. "I won't bring up your bristles by telling you why."

The expression in his eyes brought the colour surging into her cheeks and made her feel as though the world she had known were falling in pieces about her feet. She found herself unable to do other than cling to his hands in a perfectly idiotic fashion, and to say somewhat incoherently, "I do trust you won't act foolishly."

"That's past praying for, but I don't intend doing anything so very terrible," he said, smiling. But she saw he was looking at her searchingly, and thought that for an instant he had meant to kiss her. Their eyes did meet fleetingly when he raised her fingers to his lips, but before she could collect her scattered wits he had crossed to the door. "Get your things together. I will return for you at three," he added, and went out of the room.

Jessica listened to his step receding down the hall, her cheeks rosy as the meaning behind his parting words became very plain to her. The effect of this realization left her trembling, for unlike many of her gently-born contemporaries, she had retained her common sense. The gentlemen of her acquaintance might admire her beauty, but, so far as she had been able to detect, this admiration had never been attended by any burning desire to bind themselves to a penniless girl. So, far from being discontent, she had never imagined marriage to be her ultimate destiny. The prospect came, therefore, as a surprise, and put her thoughts in quite unaccustomed disorder. Feeling calm reflection necessary, she sank back in her chair to think over all that had transpired.

She could only marvel at herself, now that it came down to it. She did not appear to be put all on end, as she supposed she should be, at being skillfully drawn from her initial disjointed incredulity at the idea of marriage, to acceptance of it. She had never been in love, and while she had indulged in youthful dreams based more or less on girlish fancy, she had long known that marriage more frequently began with only the most minimal degree of affection, if indeed the participants enjoyed more than the barest acquaintance. She herself had had no notion of settling for the safe and comfortable.

So what had come over her, she wondered, dwelling on the words exchanged with Acton. She should have remained steadfast in her refusal to accede to his demands, or at the very least she should have cut short the visit, instead of which she had stood about bandying words with him, and enjoying it, she had to admit. Nothing could be more gratifying than the realization that he had enjoyed their banter every bit as much as she. The thought drew a smile to her lips, for it seemed improbable to the point of absurdity that Acton, once they were married, would conduct himself with propriety. He would cut up her peace, and argue with her ruthlessly, and life with him would be exhilarating.

CHAPTER II

Gentlemen garbed in the latest mode escorted equally fashionable ladies across the hall and up the broad staircase to the brilliantly lighted salons of Acton House. The rooms filled speedily, a footman's voice rolling forth names in rapid succession as the Polite World moved forward to pay homage to the future Duchess of Acton. Jessica curtsied for the hundredth time, her startled gaze flitting from Acton's face to that of the exquisite bowing over her hand. Casting a deprecating glance over his vacuous countenance, she wondered how this hapless creature could possibly be his Grace's heir. For that gentleman, a veritable Tulip sadly inclined to fat, had arrayed himself in a bright yellow coat with enormous mother-of-pearl buttons, worn over an elaborately embroidered short waistcoat. Pale yellow smallclothes over clocked silk stockings were clipped at the knee with ribbon-rosettes and ended in shoes adorned with huge metal buckles. The care he had bestowed upon his person, although the disdainful might suffer from a boorish want of the niceties of dress, nevertheless found favor in his own exquisite appreciation of the elegance expected from a gentleman of his standing. My Lord McClean Alastair, the Duke's cousin and a shocking tattlebox, had elected not to set every gossiping tongue awagging by displaying his chagrin before the ton.

The news of the betrothal had shocked him deeply. Rarely of late had he considered the possibility of such an event, thinking Acton securely insular to any intention of reforming his way of life. It should have been a safe thing regardless, for what doting mother bent on finding a respectable husband for her daughter would settle for a man of Acton's indefensible reputation? It would never do. He might be a Duke but he was a profligate, and shockingly ineligible. He did not scruple to disgrace the family name, nor to treat his heir in a disdainful manner.

McClean could not help feeling resentful. As if raven curls and deep blue eyes were not enough, Acton needs must have the profile of his father. His resentment found relief in plaintive speech. "I should have thought," he said, "considering the nature of our relationship, that I would have been the first informed of your intention to enter the state of matrimony. This betrothal—is it necessary?"

"No," replied his Grace, surveying him patiently. "It is agreeable—charmingly so. You may felicitate me, McClean."

"Oh, very well," McClean said crossly. "I wish you happiness." Turning to Jessica, he added with a hint of a sneer in his voice, "May I congratulate you, my lady?"

"I do wish," Acton intervened, "that you rid yourself of the notion that Jessica is to be congratulated. I reserve that honor for myself. You must not think I mean to get rid of you, dear boy, but I would recommend you seek the refreshment tables. You don't look at all the thing, you know, and there is nothing like a little food to set one up."

"If I seem a trifle off-colour, cousin, it is your lack of feeling for my sensibilities that has put me off. Oh, it is not unlike your usual conduct, but you could have thought of the descent, I should think."

"But I have, dear boy. I have," Acton returned with grave amusement. "Do you doubt it?"

"I may not be a perfect judge in such matters," McClean said stiffly, "but I cannot favour this marriage. I very much doubt—"

"—that I am worthy of my intended? You are quite correct, McClean. Jessica is very much too good for me. But don't let that concern you. If she is willing to toss her hat over the rainbow, who are we to cavil?"

There came an uncomfortable silence. McClean stared at Acton and saw not the least hint of a smile lingering in those eyes; nor could he feel at ease with the alarming grimness about the set of that handsome mouth. McClean ran the tip of his tongue over suddenly dry lips. "I did not in the least mean—pray, don't take offense—" To his very great relief, the fiddlers struck up at that moment and Acton turned away to lead Jessica to their place at the head of the line.

Some time later it seemed to Jessica that the rooms were very much more crowded. She had lost count of the number of gentlemen partnering her in the dance, and frankly enjoyed the attention she was receiving without for one moment believing the exaggerated compliments heaped upon her. Acton, watching, moved forward, only to find Lord Ames before him. "Well, John," exclaimed his friend, clapping him on the back. "So you are deserting the single state. I understand it's a desperate step to take, but having met the cause, I don't mind telling you I'm envious."

This extraordinary speech left Jessica gasping, but Acton merely drawled, "You needn't be distraught, Jules. I'm not."

"I'm not distraught, old boy. I'm grieved. The town won't seem the same without you."

"You'll just have to struggle along as best you can, I'm afraid," Acton grinned.

"That won't be for any length of time, more's the pity," Lord Ames admitted ruefully. "Papa is becoming confoundedly insistent in his strictures of late."

"We all must go eventually," Acton sympathized. "Tell me, Jules, when may we expect the publishing of your banns?"

"Plague take it, I haven't picked the chit as yet." Turning to Jessica, he audaciously asked, "Do you happen to own a twin sister, ma'am?"

"I'm sorry, no," Jessica said, enthralled.

"Run along and find your own girl," Acton chuckled, leading Jessica away to the dance floor. "This one's taken."

Whirling about the room in his arms, Jessica heard scarcely more of the music than she had the first time he danced with her. How was it, she wondered, that she had not realized the devastating effect he would have on her senses? He disturbed her as she would not have thought possible. Feeling the brush of his hard body against her soft curves as they moved over the floor, she shivered.

"Are you chilled?" he immediately leaned forward to inquire.

"I'm fine," she murmured, and shivered again at the touch of his hand upon her waist.

Concerned, he led her from the floor to seat her beside his grandmother and drape a shawl about her shoulders. "Better?" he inquired, settling down in a chair beside her.

The Dowager Duchess, unaware of Jessica's perturbation, drew their attention to a group of latecomers just entering the room. "Will you look at that gown on the Countess of Tuensdale!" she exclaimed in reproving tones. "I should think she would have better sense. But who can that be with her? Why, it's—" Glancing at Jessica, she hastily added, "Never mind."

Jessica, following the direction of her eyes, turned to Acton. "Who is the lady in the purple gown?" she asked curiously.

He looked across the room and stiffened. "A chance acquaintance," he muttered, avoiding Jessica's eyes.

"She seems to be—staring at me. But perhaps I'm mistaken."

"I'm certain you are," he answered, rising in some relief at the approach of Lord Benchley. But he was not to escape so easily. Watching Jessica go off on Benchley's arm, he heard a "Hmph!" and turned his head to look down into his grandmother's censorious eyes. "What can Lady Stanley be thinking of?" she said disapprovingly.

Feeling defeated, he sank back onto his chair. "I didn't invite her," he said shortly. "I'm not that depraved."

"You may be somewhat wild at times, Acton, but I can't think you would wish your mistress at your nuptial ball."

"She's not my mistress. At least, not now."

"Well, and I should think not. What would you want with her in your bed when you can have Jessica?" demanded Grandmama with the appalling bluntness that had long been a hallmark of her own generation.

"Yes, I know," he murmured, gazing with indulgence, and not the least surprise, upon his grandmother.

The Dowager Duchess was a tiny lady but managed to convey an impression of a much larger stature. Her white hair was curled and primped and piled high atop her head, and long diamond earrings dangled from her ears. A number of chokers and bracelets with diamonds and pearls encircled her thin neck and arms. Seldom, thought Acton, much entertained, had he seen so much jewelry worn at one time.

"I'm glad you have at last come to your senses," she began without preamble. "I knew you must someday realize your duty to the family. I want to hold my great-grandson in my arms before I die."

"I am afraid it is not that kind of marriage, Grandmama."

"Don't think I mean to interfere. I dote on you, as you well know. But I'm a nosy old busybody, so I'll give you this advice. Take your bride to bed at the first opportunity."

Acton made a choking sound in his throat. "It's obvious you haven't learned much of Jessica in the weeks she has been under your roof."

"Independent little chit, isn't she?"

"Oh, very. At any rate, she took me in instant dislike upon our first meeting. You will know I have since refrained from remarks that would put her all on end."

The Dowager Duchess digested this before directing an admonitory look at him. "I still say it would behoove you to start out in the way you mean to go on."

"You will oblige me, Grandmama, by abandoning a subject which I consider to be extremely improper."

She looked at him searchingly, trying to read his mind. The thought that he might be a stickler when it came to his betrothed had not previously occurred to her. She took a moment to think this over, and said, finally, "You are as straight-laced as any churchman, my boy. I have always thought your public pose a hum."

But he only laughed. "I trust you will not spread such heresy abroad," he murmured, the devil in his smiling eyes.

"Who would believe it?" she shot back, her expression very much the same as his. "Well, run along now, Acton. I see Benchley is taking leave of Jessica."

She was indeed rising from her curtsy. Hurrying across to Acton, she said, "Oh, I am so thankful that is over. Do not, I beg you, go away and leave me alone."

"As bad as that?" he asked, his hand holding hers reassuringly. "You seemed to find something to talk about."

"He was telling me how to go on among these people. I think he enjoyed pointing out the gentlemen whose attentions I should be wise to avoid."

Acton looked startled. "Whose idea was that?" he asked with the glimmer of a smile.

"Well, I told him I was fairly new to town—really Acton, I had to think of something. He seemed so— amorous."

He had to laugh. "Poor Benchley," he said. "We shan't tell him. It would break his heart. He fancies himself quite the ladies' man, you know."

"And well he might have been—several years ago.

I'm sorry people stared so at us. Have I made a cake of myself?"

"You haven't," he assured her gravely. "My good girl, there isn't a designing mama in the room who doesn't envy you. Do you not realize you kept England's most elusive bachelor by your side the better part of twenty minutes?"

"Well, as to that, I am sure it was because of you. If you don't mind, Acton, I would very much like a lemonade."

Enjoying himself hugely, for her innocence of these matters was something quite new in his experience, he offered his arm and led her to the refreshment room. Signaling to a footman, he waited until she had her cooling drink before he said, "Are you enjoying yourself?"

"Immensely, but I have earned a moment's rest. It was kind of you to give this ball for me."

"I wanted to present you to society myself. Don't look so surprised, Jessica. You will be my Duchess quite soon, you know."

"Yes, the time has flown, has it not? And Grandmama has kept me busy, I assure you. Scarcely an item possible to a lady's wardrobe has escaped her notice. I should never have allowed her to supervise my trousseau."

"I should have warned you," he said chuckling. "She took me along shopping once. I will never forget the experience."

"Exhausted you? I can scarce credit it. The strong male succumbing to weakness?"

"The male succumbs to many forms of weakness, my dear."

Startled, Jessica searched her mind. "I am so re-

lieved to be free of my stepfather, Acton. I cannot
express my gratitude—"

"Do not attempt to do so, I beg you. It is I who
should express such sentiments."

"Perhaps you will permit me my thoughts?"

"What male ever understood the workings of the
female mind?" he grinned, pleased to have the final
word for once.

McClean, standing close enough to overhear, looked
at them sharply, not at all pleased with the growing
affection he detected in their voices. Putting down his
glass, he strolled forward. "Am I to be allowed no
time with my new cousin-to-be?" he asked, the smirk
on his lips not quite reaching his eyes.

Acton turned his head and surveyed him with thinly
veiled hostility. "Oh—McClean," he said.

"You must not think you can monopolize her attention, Acton. Your relatives have rights too, you know."
Something that wasn't pleasant seemed to cross his
face but was gone so swiftly that Jessica thought she
must have been mistaken, for at once he was smiling.

Acton, seeing her imperceptible nod, rose. "If you
need me, I will be in the card room," he told her, and
departed.

"We will not miss him unduly, I believe," McClean
remarked, taking the chair just vacated by Acton.
"You don't strike me as the sort to remain faithful to
any man."

Jessica stared at him in complete amazement. "You
are insolent, sir," she breathed, finally, in measured
tones.

"Are you so unapproachable? I wonder," he
drawled, a chilling look in his eyes. "A beautiful
woman is made for love. And you are very beautiful."

"Even a pink of the ton such as yourself might accord one the barest civility. But perhaps you have not known many gentlewomen?"

"I'll forgive your unkind words, m'dear, for I'm constrained to think you do not mean them." He studied her angry face. "What a pair we would make," he mused enigmatically. "I wonder if you are worth the risk."

"If Acton were here, you would not speak in this fashion. If you do not leave, I will inform him."

"You disappoint me, cousin-to-be. I would have expected a more original threat from your adorable lips." He waved a bloodless hand about. "All this will one day be mine. You could do worse than be—kind to me."

Jessica gasped, the colour suffusing her face. Rising to her feet in one graceful movement, she hurried toward the card room, willing herself not to run, and nearly collided with Acton. "Here!" he exclaimed, startled. "Is something amiss?"

"No," she replied with hard-fought calm. "Nothing of the sort. I was looking for you, that is all." The minutes that had ticked by in reaching his side had brought her excellent counsel. McClean's insults were not, after all, so very bad—rather childish, truly.

Lord Ames, at this moment catching sight of them, brought his companion over. "Really, Richard, you must show it to Lady Cooke," he said gayly, as Jessica curtsied to Lord Lester. "I know she will be entranced with it."

"Oh, it is adorable," she cried, gazing at the tiny object attached to his lordship's fob chain. "Why, it's a carving of a little fat man!"

"Chinese," explained Lord Lester.

"Ch'ien-lung," unerringly stated Acton.

"Quite correct," agreed Lord Lester. "Theme: the deity Chen Wu, in ivory."

"Oh, no," groaned Lord Ames in mock dismay. "They will go on prosing forever on a subject we know nothing about. Shall we leave them together, Lady Cooke, while we join the dance?"

"Indeed we shall," she smiled, sinking into a curtsy before Acton, down and down, as to Royalty. Rising, her skirts swaying gracefully, she pertly cocked her head. "If you will excuse me, your Grace?"

Not to be outdone, Acton bowed with consummate charm, and raised her fingers to his lips. "One dance only, Jules," he said to Lord Ames as he left the room with Jessica.

Observing this episode, Lady Stanley stood framed in the doorway, the careful pose of her body portraying every line of her exquisitely proportioned figure. The low décolletage of her gown revealing rather than concealing her bosom caught all masculine attention as she moved forward to smile entrancingly upon her quarry. "Good evening, Acton," she trilled. "Are you glad to see me?"

"It is an unexpected pleasure."

"I had to see you," she said quickly, conscious of the disapproval in his eyes.

"You should never have come," he answered in tones she could only think dry.

"Oh, la," she shrugged. "As if I care what the biddies say. 'Pon rep, but I shouldn't expect pretense from you, of all people."

"I was thinking of you."

She gave a quick sigh. "Sometimes I think you forget all about me when I'm not with you."

His smile seemed cynical. "How could I?" he murmured after a slight pause. "Gentlemen always remember beautiful ladies."

"That is not what I meant, as you very well know. It has been so long, Acton."

There came a pregnant silence. "I hesitate to speak indelicately, Imogene, but I must ask the present whereabouts of Lord Stanley."

"I'm sure I wouldn't know. He doesn't interfere with me, nor I with him. You've always known that, Acton."

"I dislike blunt speaking, Imogene, but I'm very much afraid I must ask you to leave."

Leaning forward, she murmured too softly for Lord Lester to overhear, "I could return after everyone has gone."

"Behave yourself," he admonished, ignoring the longing in her eyes which she made no attempt to conceal.

Fortunately for Acton, McClean's predilection for mischief served him well in this instance, for that cousin now materialized at his elbow. "I trust, Acton," he said unpleasantly, "that you are prepared to explain this untidy little contretemps to your fiancée?"

Acton did not seem daunted. "Am I to understand you are offering to immolate yourself on the altar of hymeneal piety?"

"You may be pleased to sneer at me, but it is only fair to tell you that I shall not assist you out of your difficulty." McClean drew himself up short. Acton was not in this instance his quarry; he had likelier game in mind. The Lady Jessica adorned the dance; it would please him mightily to make Acton's mistress known to her. Achieving (to his mind) a beautiful leg, he smiled upon Lady Stanley. "Will you honour me by standing up with me for the next set, m'dear?

The music is lively, and I have a surprise in store."

"Really?" she said, her interest caught. "What is it?"

"Tut tut, no hints now," he smirked, holding out his arm.

Acton watched without expression as they moved away before turning his head to smile upon his friend. "Speak, Richard," he said, "before you choke on your own restraint."

Lord Lester chuckled. "I swear, dear boy, I was but intending to extend my sympathy."

"You are most generous."

"One's bird has an unhappy way of returning to the dovecote, eh? Even one given the bye-bye months ago. Well, buck up, old boy. I will contrive to remove Lady Stanley from the premises before she runs afoul of Lady Cooke."

"Between the two of us, Richard, I'm getting too old for this sort of thing."

"At twenty-nine? Come, John." Seeing Jessica returning on the arm of Lord Ames, Lord Lester grinned. "I think your youth is about to be restored," he said, and went in search of Lady Stanley.

"You have an incomparable on your hands," Lord Ames remarked to Acton as he turned Jessica over to him.

She was taken aback for a moment. She knew herself to be a success, but laid it at his Grace's door. It was his title and wealth, she didn't doubt. "I do not care a snap for that," she said somewhat crossly.

Acton looked at her with a worried frown. "Are you weary, Jessica?" he asked in concern before leading to a settee.

"I'm worn out," she admitted, sinking down gracefully onto the soft cushions. "Do you think anyone would notice if I took off my slippers?"

"Not if you contrive to keep them under your skirts," he assured her, eyes shining. "Will you need help in removing them?"

"No," she gasped, cheeks suddenly pink. "I can manage, thank you." Acton sat gazing down at her in delight, much entertained by the odd, agitated movements taking place under her skirts. Succeeding at last in kicking off the offending gear, she peeped down to make sure they were tucked safely out of sight, and leaned back in contentment. "Ah," she sighed, and wiggled her toes.

"If all these people weren't around, I would kiss you," his voice murmured in her ear. "The impulse is strong, believe me."

Her eyes flew to his. "And so we begin," she said.

"Where we are like to end."

Jessica, chagrined at having him take her up so quickly, flushed. "How very shabby of you," she said. "I left myself open for that, didn't I?"

He burst out laughing. "Let that be a lesson to you. I have no scruples, you see."

"If we had not your shocking manners to discuss, we would have nothing to talk about."

"I should have known I wouldn't clear that hurdle without a fall. I must remember to say only what I ought."

That drew a chuckle from her. "Don't set a clamp on your tongue on my account. You should start out in the way you mean to go on."

Recalling these exact words from Grandmama, and their context, he gave a shout of laughter. "May I share the joke?" Lord Ames asked, coming up to them.

"Go away, Jules," gasped his Grace.

"I only came to tell you your guests are leaving."

"Oh, dear," Jessica murmured, groping around with

her feet for her slippers. "Oh, dear," she murmured
again as one of them popped into view.

"You seem to have lost a shoe," Lord Ames remarked, gazing down in surprise upon the wandering
offender.

"There is nothing for it, you need help." Acton
grinned, kneeling before her, the shoe in hand. Jessica, mortified, put out her foot. "Now the other one,"
he said, and waited until she pushed it forward.

Rising, she placed her hand on Lord Ames's arm.
"Some gentlemen have the grace to turn their heads,"
she said.

"Some gentlemen are not your intended," Acton
chuckled, tucking her other hand in his. "Jules is
welcome to tag along. I have no complaint to make.
No complaint at all."

CHAPTER III

The towering twin gate posts, with their bronze metal eagles, were left behind, and the chaise continued on along the tree-lined drive. Jessica withdrew her gaze from massed rhododendron and ran an indignant eye over Acton's slumbering form. Insufferable, she thought. He need only close his eyes. You may be sure he had forgotten her very existence. Feeling a little envious, and every bit as weary, she turned her head and resumed a somewhat desultory scrutiny of the landscape. It was interesting enough, with a woodland giving way to grasslands dotted with grazing sheep, but Jessica, very much in the way of ordering things as she chose, would have preferred Acton awake.

It had been an exhausting day, dawning clear and bright, and a softness in the air made it seem perfect weather for a wedding. Leaves had quietly rustled in the breeze, gently casting their dappled shade upon the walks, to mingle with soft music majestically flowing on the air through the open portals of the church. A hush had fallen as the organ burst into the

strains of the wedding march, but Acton, waiting beside the altar, had scarcely glanced at the procession
approaching down the aisle. His gaze had been fastened on the opening through which she would appear on the arm of Lord Ames.

Her silver-embroidered gown had brushed the floor,
its long train sweeping behind her, the heavily en-
crusted bodice hugging her rounded breasts and nip-
ping her waist, while full skirts flared about her
slender form. Kneeling by his side, she had felt com-
forted by the service, and quite unprepared for the
thrill that shot through her when, at the conclusion
of the ceremony, he lifted her veil and lightly pressed
his lips to hers.

"You have my permission to rest your head on my
shoulder," came his lazy voice beside her, interrupting
her reverie.

Startled, Jessica turned her head, to look full into
his softened gaze. "I believe I won't, thank you," she
managed, striving to marshal her wayward thoughts.

A look of amusement crossed his face. "I am more
than sorry, my dear. I should have liked it excessively.
Are you quite certain you won't change your mind?"

She laughed. "You have a surplus of rakish notions
in your head, your Grace."

"Why, oh why, could we not have met years ago?"
he returned, a glint in his eyes.

"Because years ago I was sewing my samplers while
you were busily acquiring your shocking reputation."

His lips twitched. "Does my reputation shock you?"
he asked gravely.

"Not at all," she replied composedly. "I have always
wanted to know a man with libertine propensities. I
have heard much of them, but, until you, I hadn't run

across one. In general my life has been rather dull, but I see that will now be quite at an end."

He gave a shout of laughter. "Good God, does that mean I am to initiate you into a life of debauchery?"

"Well, I don't quite understand what that is, but it wouldn't be reasonable to expect you to change. It will be much better if I join you. Tell me, Acton. Just what is a life of debauchery? I have heard of a life of sin, but I don't know whether they are the same."

At this entirely unexpected speech, he half turned in his seat to gaze at her, first with incredulity, then with a hint of inquiry. As she met his look, a flush crept into her cheeks. "Have I said something I oughtn't?" she asked.

"No, but I can't explain it to you."

"You can't? Then I'll just have to find out for myself. How much farther is it to Aynesworth?"

"We have been on the estate since we turned in at the gates."

Jessica was shocked. How could she possibly be mistress to such an establishment! The bowing couple by the gate posts was now identified (the lodge keeper and his wife), and must be only the first of the servants who would cross her path. Jessica surmised that there would be quite a number more. She came closer to the truth than she realized—there proved to be a virtual army of them lined up in welcome once they entered the hall.

For her part, she considered the house a perfect example of its kind. Set in a valley between two forests, and surrounded by terraces descending to a lake, the Elizabethan mansion was built of a pinkish stone, its huge Corinthian-topped pilasters reaching toward a roof adorned with carved stone sculptures.

According to the *Traveler's Guide,* a villa reputed to have been the summer residence of a Roman general had once occupied the site, though historians readily admitted that the Alastairs themselves made no such claim.

"Are you weary? Yes, of course you are," Acton said, taking her across the marble hall. "May I suggest a rest before dinner?"

This programme met with her instant approval. "I must own I was afraid you might not suggest it," she admitted with a great deal of relief. "You did nap on the way here, you know."

"While you did not." He grinned, and, before she had time to realize his intent, scooped her up in his arms and calmly carried her up the stairs.

Jessica turned beet-red. She knew the servants were gaping at them from the hall, so she didn't dare struggle; as soon as they reached the floor above, however, she requested he set her on her feet, only to feel his arms tighten their hold. She wanted to slap him. She managed not to do it, and even smiled, since it was evident that a slap would only provide the servants with a further spectacle to titter about.

That, as it happened, quickly became the least of her worries. For Acton carried her into her apartment and kicked the door closed with his heel. "Thank you. You may put me down," she then said.

Cutting his eyes wickedly at her, he strode across her sitting room to her bedroom beyond. "Here we are, my dear," he said, chuckling. "Do you like it?"

"Blue is my favorite colour," she answered cautiously, gazing around while contriving not to look into those eyes so very close to her own.

"It is?" he asked in surprise. "Mine also," he added with satisfaction, while slowly lowering her to her feet.

Jessica despised the flush again invading her cheeks at the feel of her soft body brushing along his strong, lean frame. She stood in the center of the Aubusson carpet and looked around, very conscious of the huge four-poster bed that seemed, in her flustered state, to fill the room. It looked inviting, and she wondered what it would be like . . .

She favoured rococo design and felt the soft blue of damask drapery perfect against grey walls. Only too conscious of his eyes upon her, she crossed to the Chippendale mirror over a French commode and removed her bonnet. "The pictures are interesting," she remarked for something to say.

"I'm happy you noticed. Great-grandmother painted them."

She glanced at him in surprise and strolled around, inspecting them closely, consuming more time in the process than perhaps was warranted. "They are quite good," she said at last.

"Come and see my room," his voice murmured in her ear, so close she gave a little jump. Placing his arm about her waist to urge her through a connecting door, he waited for her comment.

"How nice," she faltered, trying not to notice the huge bed with its crested canopy. It seemed to her that beds were all she had seen since entering the house.

"Shall we see if our tea is laid?" he finally suggested. "I find that I am hungry."

Jessica, settling herself to pour, wondered if he were as conscious of the beds as she, and thought that very probably he was. "It is good to be home," he remarked as he accepted his plate from her. "It's been an exhausting day. We will retire early."

"I am anxious to see all of Aynesworth," she replied, searching her mind for a safer topic to introduce into

the conversation. "We could bespeak an early breakfast and then set out on our tour. When we became
engaged, I made it my business to read about the
house. Do you know, Acton, it is really quite famous."

"I have no doubt it is, but I have not the least desire
to rise at an early hour in the morning," he murmured
provocatively. "Neither, I might add, will you."

"We could start now, could we not?" she said hesitantly, not quite able to meet his eyes. "I am anxious
to explore it."

"And so you shall, of course. But not tonight," he
hastily added. "We would never get to bed." His eyes
went a very dark blue indeed as his thoughts veered
to the hours ahead. He took her hands in his to assist
her to her feet, then turned his head in annoyance as
a tap sounded on the door.

"Excuse me, your Grace," a red-faced footman stammered. "But g-guests have just arrived."

"Guests!" Acton ejaculated, thunderstruck. "What
the devil—" Clamping his lips together, he gritted,
"We will be down presently," and dismissed the footman with a nod.

"Your friends have little discrimination, it seems,"
Jessica remarked the moment they were alone. "I can't
think where you met them."

"Water seeks its own level," he retorted, in the grip
of extreme and perfectly understandable frustration.
"It does seem a pity you should learn the truth about
me after such a promising start, but then, life is full
of disappointments."

"As bad as that?" she said sympathetically. "Always
remember, your Grace, that one is judged by the
company one keeps."

"I'm beginning to understand how a man could become a misogynist." Crossing to the door, he held it

open for her to precede him. "Shall we join our guests, Jessie?" he said.

She recoiled. "What did you call me?" she demanded, an angry flush mounting to her cheeks.

He put up his brows. "Isn't that your name?" he purred. "The marriage registry says it is."

"You would!" she said, turning to face him defiantly under the glow of candlelight. He made no reply, but stood staring, the heat rising up in him at the sight of soft light tinging her cheeks with rose. Jessica remained quite still, the expression in his eyes conjuring up a vision of marriage so appealing she found she must forcibly put it from her mind. She regretted the interruption every bit as much as he did. Suddenly finding the use of her limbs, she preceded him out of the room.

Acton, easily reading her thoughts, felt the ire rise in his breast at the sight that greeted his eyes as they descended the stairs. The hall rang with the sounds of people laughing and calling to one another while the butler directed footmen in the disposition of cloaks and capes. Saunders looked, in all truth, as harassed as Acton himself felt.

"Acton, darling," Jessica heard a voice trill, and turned to see a glowing creature separate herself from the others to fling her arms about his neck. She had no trouble at all recognizing the lady who had attended her nuptial ball in a purple gown.

Acton stared stunned by vision pressing against his chest. "Imogene! My God!" he gasped, his hands reaching for her wrists to remove her arms.

"That's Imo for you," one of the gentlemen laughed, shoving Lady Stanley aside to grasp Acton by the hand. "She's a shameless hussy, isn't she?"

"Quentin! What are you doing here?" Acton demanded, aghast.

"Just dropped in, old boy. Just dropped in."

"George. You too?"

"Sure thing. I couldn't let them come without me."

It was a fashionable group surging about his Grace, the ladies gay and chic in the latest styles, the gentlemen the epitome of fashion. One of these latter suddenly exclaimed, "And what have we found in your nest, Acton? A fledgling ripe for the plucking."

Acton glared murderously at the offender. "Dare to touch her—" he spat before pushing his way through the now silent group to Jessica's side. "I am honoured to present my wife, her Grace, the Duchess of Acton," he said, leading her forward.

"Your wife! Oh, I say—"

Jessica read surprise, astonishment, wonder in their faces. In the Lady Imogene's she saw venom.

"We hadn't heard of your marriage," Lord Quentin told Acton, a worried frown between his eyes. "Wouldn't have barged in, you know. We have been in Wales for the hunt, then went by Froggie's boat to Brighton."

"I tried to get in touch with you, but no one knew where to find either you or George. You would, of course, have been invited to the wedding."

"Sorry to have missed it. When was it, by the way?"

"It was—recent! We have just arrived from London."

"Oh, Lord!" breathed Quentin. "I don't know who thought to come here."

"I did," came Imogene's voice, speaking clearly.

"You knew, didn't you?" Quentin glared at her.

"Well, as long as we're here, we might as well stay,"

said the man called Froggie. "This pile has plenty of rooms."

Into the pause that followed this rude remark, Lord Quentin turned to Jessica, an apologetic look in his eyes. "I hope we haven't put you out," he said. "We should leave."

"Do not mention it, pray," she replied, forcing a gracious smile to her lips. "We are happy to have you," she added, and excused herself to see to arrangements for their accommodation.

She consulted with the housekeeper, and decided to put the gentlemen in the west wing and the ladies in the east. She thought privately that one certain lady could well be put in the attics. Coming to a decision, she said, "The Lady Imogene Stanley shall have the rose room. It is quite the loveliest on the floor. And in the green room—" (she searched her memory for the name of the tall blond) "—Miss Lambert. The yellow room will serve as their sitting room." She was quite taken with the thought. Miss Lambert obviously was of the horsey set, quite mad for the hunt. She should succeed in irritating my Lady Imogene to a marked degree. "As for the other ladies—assign them at your discretion, Mrs. Eddywin."

There was a great deal of reluctance in Jessica's step as she returned to the drawing room. On the one hand, she was determined to make the best of the deplorable situation in which they found themselves; on the other, she had far too much sense to expect much from the gathering together of such an unlikely assortment of people. She moved silently along the hall, her step whispering along the carpet; the two persons still remaining in the salon were unaware of her approach. "I don't know, Isobel," Miss Lambert's voice said, drifting through the partially opened door. "Acton seemed to dote on her, but men are seldom faithful to their wives. At least, that has been my observation."

"Well, I think Imogene is just abominable," Isobel replied. "And besides, I thought that affair was over."

"Some men never forget a mistress. And I must say, Isobel, Imogene is the kind of woman men find irresistible."

Jessica stood as if turned to stone. Oh, dear God! she thought. I wish I had never known. Stunned, white, mortified, she turned and fled to the sanctuary of her rooms—and ran straight into the arms of Acton. "Here, what is this?" he demanded, holding her shoulders with the steel of his hands.

"You!" she hissed, attempting to jerk free. "Let me go!"

He shook her slightly. "What is it?"

"I heard those women talking. They said Lady Stanley is your mistress," she said accusingly.

Startled, he stood gazing down at her. Damn, he thought. I should have expected this. Releasing her, he crossed to take up a stance before the fire. "Jessica, a man has certain appetites. It is natural that he should. He will appease them, and there are women willing, more so if he happens to own a title and some wealth."

"Oh!" groaned Jessica, sinking down upon one of the gilt and blue satin chairs.

"You must realize that such alliances mean nothing."

"No, not to you!" she said bitterly. "Oh, I can readily believe they wouldn't."

"Until I met you, Jessica, I thought all women were grasping and greedy, ready to sell themselves to the highest bidder. But you were different. You faced marriage to a stranger defiantly, trying your best to get out of it, even though that marriage meant great wealth and one of the highest titles in the land."

"Possibly," she gritted through her teeth. "But the fact remains, you are a rake. A black-hearted, arrogant—"

"Are you searching for contemptible?"

"Thank you—contemptible despoiler of womankind. You are dissolute and unscrupulous, and henceforth, my lord Duke, your morals are no concern of mine!"

"I may be all you say, and while you may not believe I regret my past, be pleased to believe you are not the only sufferer in this marriage."

"It is a little late for regrets, though believe me, I do regret marrying you. I did marry you, however, and I am perfectly aware of my responsibilities, loathsome though they be to me. You will have no cause for complaint, your Grace, insofar as my public duties are concerned. I will appear downstairs, suitably gowned, to grace the head of your table and entertain your guests. You need have no qualms about that. And now, sir, you are at liberty to leave my rooms."

"By all that is holy, I could shake you," he said, and, turning sharply on his heel, strode from her presence, shutting the door with a snap behind him.

Two hours later Jessica was dressing for dinner, determined to outshine the other ladies. What right had anyone to assume that Lady Stanley could put her in the shade! She would wear the yellow muslin, repeating the decoration of the dining room. Recalling the roses for the table, she had Agnes pile her hair high atop her head, threading it through with

deep red ribbon. The Alastair rubies were added, and
she stood back to study the effect. Her eye catching
a movement in the long mirror, she turned to see
Acton standing on the threshold.

We might have planned it, she thought, for incred-
ibly he wore a ruby satin coat and pale yellow smallclothes. The intricately contrived folds of his cravat
held ruby studs, while ruby rings adorned his fingers.
He regarded her with irony, and said in his dryest
tones, "We seem to be of one mind. Shall we proceed
below for the edification of our guests?"

It was no easy task to face him. She hesitated, and
then with firm resolve sank into a curtsy. The only
clear thought in her head was that they looked a
handsome couple. This put her in mind of the satisfaction she would feel upon their entry into the
drawing room.

"What nonsense is this?" Lady Stanley demanded
the instant they appeared. She was wearing a gown
of scarlet satin. Hussy, thought Jessica. It was difficult to understand what held the dress in place, it
was cut so low.

"They're a smashing pair, and you know it," said
Lord Quentin, turning his back on her. "Acton must
bring you on a visit to Scotland when the heather
blooms," he said to Jessica. "It transforms the landscape and every Scot rejoices."

"I recall my first sight of it," George remarked.
"One must be impressed."

"I recall you were impressed by the Highland las-
sie you saw nearby," Quentin grinned. "George turned
up a gel at every stop, ma'am. You wouldn't believe
the unlikely places. You should take a ramble about
with him sometime."

"Oh, no," laughed Jessica. "Not if I were expected to produce the lassies. I would feel like a witch."

Lady Imogene's lip curled. "Aren't you letting out the family secrets?" she purred.

Acton stiffened. "If I leave Jessica in your care, Quentin," he said, crossing to stand by her side, "am I safe in assuming she will be safe from your blandishments?"

"Sure thing, old boy," Lord Quentin answered cheerfully. "I can't say I fancy one of your famous setdowns."

"Has Acton set you down?" Imogene asked Jessica maliciously, a syrupy smile curving her lips.

"Why, no," Jessica answered just as sweetly. "Nothing could be further from his mind."

"Really, it is all so provincial," Imogene snapped, her voice clear and cutting. "Such a change, this billing and cooing. You are become so stodgy, Acton."

His reply was prompt and cold. "You need not concern yourself," he said distinctly.

Her chime of laughter rippled, loud and jarring. "But I am concerned. This farce is so very, very—public."

He knew her well enough to ignore the remark, though he remained alert for further possible scenes. God! he thought, how could she ever have engaged his fancy? He must have been demented. And the devil of it was, Jessica had her back up, and he could not blame her for that. Imogene was much more easily dealt with.

Had any man ever before, he wondered bitterly, so spent his nuptial eve?

CHAPTER IV

Late the following morning, as she descended the
stairs, Jessica turned her thoughts to entertainment
for the guests. Perhaps they could have a picnic beside the lake, to be followed by a bathing party. And
a hunt could no doubt be arranged. Her knowledge
of their tastes was vague, limited as it was to one
evening in their company, but Acton could contrib-
ute to the plans. A few families must reside within
reach of Aynesworth, making plausible a small dinner.

As she reached the foot of the stairs, Acton came
out of the library. "I was just going to send for you,"
he said, standing aside for her to precede him into
the room.

She walked down the long length of it, conscious
of him beside her watching her every expression.
Nothing could have put her at a greater disadvantage;
she felt she might stumble at any moment, or do
something equally foolish. The thought brought her
chin up. Pausing beside a chair, she met his glance

and was startled by the frank humility in his eyes. Stubborn to a fault, she waited for him to speak.

"You may as well sit," he said with a lopsided smile. "I won't eat you."

The remark made her colour slightly. She couldn't decide why she found it impossible to answer. She only knew she felt self-conscious and slightly ridiculous. Taking the chair he indicated with a wave of his hand, she said finally, "I rose from my bed later than I intended."

"Why should you explain that to me? You may rise when you please."

"But the guests—"

"Have departed." At her look of surprise, he added ruefully, "I had hoped you would notice the quiet in the house, and be glad. I see I expected too much."

"Why did they leave?"

"To be accurate about it, I ordered Imogene and Froggie to leave. The others refused to take them up, so I sent them to the village in the estate carriage. The accommodation coach makes regular stops; they will find transport readily enough."

"Lady Stanley will never forgive you."

"I trust you aren't indulging your fancy in thinking I care whether she does or not. I simply did not intend to endure any longer the sound of her viperous tongue. As for Froggie, Aynesworth's hospitality doesn't extend that far." He cast a glance at her, and said in a constrained voice, "We have gotten off to a poor start, but it is conceivable we can again be friends."

"Do you think so? I would very much prefer not being enemies."

"I don't doubt we will quarrel, but I promise not to start it."

"Pray don't say that. How can you talk in such an exaggerated fashion? You will quarrel with me at the first opportunity."

"Just so," he said, chuckling. "I see your disapproval of me hasn't blinded you to such an extent that you don't see to a nicety how to say whatever comes into your head."

"Wretch! That was most unchivalrous of you." She tried to hold her lips primly, but failed. "Whatever I know of reprehensible speaking, sir, I have learned from you."

"For shame! And I had intended taking you riding. You haven't as yet worn your ruby habit, and it is a fine day."

"If I agree, will you behave?"

"And you have the audacity to label me a wretch," he grinned in reply, crossing to the door. "While you change, I will have the horses brought around."

Twenty mintues later, Jessica stood on the front steps observing the antics of the stallion favoured by Acton. The large chestnut, snorting and prancing in an attempt to break free from the groom clinging to the reins, wheeled to kick at stable boys scrambling for safety from the flashing hooves. Hurrying to the smaller mare, she stroked the silken nose and murmured soothingly to her. "She's lovely, Acton. Does she have a name?"

"It is Lottie."

"What an odd name for a horse."

"Blame Jenks here," he grinned, nodding toward the groom. "He named her."

The groom hung his head. "Her dam had a lot of colts, your Grace," he explained sheepishly.

Jessica gave her throaty laugh. "A most proper name, Jenks."

Acton turned to the stallion, his grin widening. "Feeling his oats, is he?"

"There's the devil in him this morning, your Grace."

The animal reared and lunged when Acton swung into the saddle and gathered the reins in an iron grip. Whinnying and tossing up pebbles with his hooves, the stallion fought the tightening reins in frustration until, finally, he stood quiet and subdued. "And what do you call him?" Jessica asked Jenks.

"Beelzebub, your Grace."

"Also aptly named," she smiled in delight.

Passing down the drive, they crossed the fields and headed for the woods and a knoll just beyond. Dismounting, Jessica strolled away to stand looking at the view, then jumped slightly when Acton, coming up behind her, put his arms around her. He drew her to lean against his strength. "As a boy I spent many hours here when I wished to be alone," he murmured, nuzzling at her nape.

"The view is outstanding," she replied nervously. "It is as if we were hanging in the sky with the earth spread out below us."

"Do you see the river curving around a hill in the distance? It is the northern boundary of Aynesworth." He sighed in content. "It is so peaceful here."

Jessica, for reasons best known to herself, disengaged his arms and strolled across to seat herself on a grassy spot. "You haven't told me of your boyhood," she said, glancing up at him.

Dropping down beside her, he leaned back, propped up on one elbow. "So we are to discuss the story of my life."

"I do not think I care to know what you were about in your later years. Just your boyhood, please."

"They tell me I put in an appearance on a Monday morning, at about six o'clock, I believe, some two weeks late. My first words were gla-gloo, and I took my first steps at about eleven months. Now let me see—"

"Acton!"

"I thought I should start at the beginning," he said innocently.

"I knew you were not born a rake," she shot back in triumph. "There must have been *some* time when you were normal—at around ten years, perhaps?"

"By that age I had lost my parents and Grandmama was in charge. You may be sure I toed the mark. So did McClean, by the way."

"He seems a rather—offensive person."

"He is, and I do not intend to tolerate his presence at Aynesworth in future."

"Is he really your heir?"

"Unfortunately, yes. Our grandfathers were half-brothers. That branch of the family has gone off sadly, I'm afraid."

Jessica was curious and eager to ask questions, for, as she now realized for the first time, she knew little of his family. Grandmama was a dear, and she had come to love her, but with the rush of accumulating her trousseau and of the wedding itself, it had not occurred to her to think of much else. She knew Acton had a sister who was increasing and unable to attend their wedding, and she wondered if other relatives he might have would resemble McClean.

"You didn't realize what you were letting yourself in for when you married me," Acton's voice broke the silence. Studying her impassively, he added, "No man finds pleasure in baring his soul, but sometimes it is advisable to do just that."

She raised startled eyes to his. "Acton, you need not—"

"As my wife you are entitled to the family secrets. But it is not a pretty story, I'm afraid." He wore an unusually sober expression on his face from wondering if his disclosures would utterly destroy what little credit he had left with her. "My great-grandfather loved his first wife dearly and she bore him several children, of which only my grandfather survived his infancy. Then my great-grandmother died quite young of some malady, and great-grandfather was wild with grief. It seems he then lost interest in his former associations. At any rate, he unexpectedly married again during a somewhat reprehensible stay in London, to a lady of doubtful background, from all accounts. Society refused to receive her and she retired to Aynesworth."

"I'm sorry," Jessica said, not knowing what else to say.

"No need to be. Such things do happen. Great-grandfather did not live with this second wife for any length of time, preferring the company of his cronies in London." Turning his head, he gazed at her. "Rumors of that day hinted of strange behavior on her part. In fact, Jessica, Grandmama has told me she was thought at the time to be unstable. There may have been a grain of truth in that, for her son was certainly odd in his behaviour. He held the view that my grandfather had cheated him out of inheriting the dukedom. This son, Ernest, was McClean's grandfather, by the way."

"But how could he possibly think that? The eldest son always inherits."

"Yes, but he had the warped idea that my grandfather was illegitimate. Grandmama thinks his mother may have planted the seed in his brain."

Jessica gazed thoughtfully at him, and said, finally, "Perhaps she *was* unstable."

"That may have been true. Or it may have been a misguided maternal instinct to promote the prospects of her own son. Whatever the reason, Ernest spent his life searching for proof of this obsession. I have wondered at times if his wife did not become infected with the same delusion. You have yet to meet my great-aunt Eurice." He glanced at her, and said with some humour, "I seem to have a surplus of somewhat questionable relations."

"While I, sir, have only relatives of the highest order to recommend me."

"You would be hard put to equal mine, I assure you," he murmured, sitting up and putting an arm around her shoulders. "My dislike of McClean comes from his running into debt in anticipation of the inheritance. In any event, I have become confoundedly exasperated with bailing him out of his difficulties. I informed him there will be no further monies from me in future."

"Did he believe you?"

"He is a fool if he did not."

Jessica's mind began to wander, reeling with the nearness of him, his masculine good looks, the strength of his body. She found she had to force herself to remember that he had a mistress. It might prove difficult, this holding him at bay.

She became aware of an irrational and almost overwhelming impulse to run her fingers through his hair. She subdued it, and spoke with deliberation. "Well, I'm sure that is up to you. And now, I will ask you to release me. I can't make you, as you very well know, for my strength is less than yours." She looked at him searchingly, and saw the rebellion in his eyes. "I know you did not actually promise to behave, but I assumed you would. Am I also to assume you are not to be trusted?"

He was taken aback, and, while an angry flush suffused his face, he did remove his arms. "Your tongue is scissors-sharp," he remarked, his eyes narrowing.

"If this is any indication of the way you mean to conduct yourself, we shall certainly end up as enemies," she retorted. "I daresay you would prefer I turn my back on your mistress, but you aren't that well acquainted with me, after all. I don't know how many such females have fallen victim to your charms, nor do I care, but I won't so easily succumb."

"I was mistaken. You have the tongue of a serpent."

"Am I to understand, then, that if I speak more sweetly, you will molest me? How chivalrous."

"No," he said mockingly. "It isn't your tongue that will put me off. The nastiness of your disposition will. I trust we now understand one another?"

"But, of course, your Grace," she answered just as mockingly, despising herself for it, but unable to stop herself. "Perhaps you should pursue Lady Stanley. Hotfoot, as it were."

"If I don't someday wring your precious little neck, it won't be from want of reason."

"Then I must take care not to run risks." Rising, she shook out her skirts, and crossed to the mare.

"You have nothing to fear. I shan't touch you," he tossed at her back as she rode off. "And she hasn't been my mistress for six months," he fairly shouted at her retreating form.

CHAPTER V

Imogene, with little enough to occupy her time, turned her head slightly on the faded squabs of the accommodation coach and surveyed her traveling companions with repugnance. The stout woman in the seat across from her slumped in sleep, with mouth open and jaw sagging, a trace of the food she had consumed clinging to her chin. Imogene wrinkled her nose in disgust, and glared at Froggie, himself sprawled in a corner and asleep. Jostled about by the swaying of the cumbersome vehicle, she settled herself as comfortably as she might, and gave herself over to thoughts of Acton.

He could not be enamoured of that silly chit, a doxy won at gaming. He enjoyed a jolly time, with gaiety and clever companionship, and must be restored to reason. The problem lay in finding a way to discredit Jessica to such a marked degree that he would find her company degrading. Could she be induced to behave in such an outrageous manner as to disgust him? On reflection, Imogene was forced to abandon the thought. Jessica would be unlikely to do so. If she would commit no blunder of her own volition then, some action must be forced upon her. Perhaps the person enroute to meet with them could supply the answer.

Imogene was roused from these musings by the coach lurching to a standstill, and she looked out of the window to see the vague shape of an inn looming in the murky dark. No light shone forth to indicate human habitation. "Are you quite certain this is Agecroft?" she asked the guard the moment he pulled open the door. Receiving the surliest of nods for answer could scarcely afford her gratification. The place looked none too savory, and in all probability she would find herself the only female present. Picking up her reticule from the seat beside her, she took the hand held out by the guard and stepped down from the coach.

The entrance to the Hare and Hounds opened into a tiny hall, with a swinging lantern that gave off only enough light to penetrate the gloom. An opening to one side afforded the travelers a glimpse of the common room, an uninviting chamber whose sole illumination appeared to originate from its blackened fireplace. Imogene thought it just as well the light was dim; she doubted they would find the place palatable in the daylight. Seated on a long bench with beer on the scarred table before her, for the inn could provide no likelier beverage, she leaned toward Froggie, her voice beguiling.

"I have been considering how best to repay Acton for his cavalier treatment of us, and have asked myself what he would hold most dear. The answer is, of course, Jessica's virtue. He is a proud man, Froggie. Take that from him and we destroy him."

Froggie's jaw dropped. "Have you taken leave of your senses?" he exclaimed in tones of profound disbelief.

"Please do not waste our time with needless protestations," she said shortly. "Acton must be brought to his senses if he is to return to me."

He glanced at her, amazed. For a woman wise in the ways of men, she was lamentably vulnerable in her obsession with this one. Acton was obviously so enraptured of his bride that Imogene must be blind not to see. The only wonder of it was that her presence had been tolerated at Aynesworth, however briefly. Aloud, he said, "You are taking your own good time in coming to the point."

"The point, my dear Froggie, is that Acton's treatment of you should obviate any scruples you might harbour concerning Jessica's virtue. As the injured party, the privilege must belong to you. Need I be more explicit?"

"You mean you expect me—" he sputtered, dumbfounded.

"I cannot conceive why you should mind. She is not unattractive."

"But I never thought of her in that way."

"Then I suggest you contrive to do so."

"You must be mad. We would never escape Acton's vengeance."

Into the silence that greeted this remark, a simpering voice drawled from the doorway. "What are you conspiring about?" its owner asked.

Imogene turned her head, to glare at the newcomer. "You took your own good time in arriving," she shot back acidly.

No lady of innate honesty, and Jessica was a lady of

considerable honesty, could spend a vexing day, followed by an even more trying night, without admitting to herself the cause of her distress. The reason, in vulgar parlance, stood well over six feet in height, and needed taking down a peg. Just why this was so, she came around to acknowledging at about the time the sun put in its appearance for the day. But what to do about it did not occur to her until long after she had risen from her bed. My lord Duke would be made to realize that the favours of a wife could far exceed those of any mistress, including, most certainly, a discarded one. She wouldn't be bested by Lady Stanley.

It had been her intention to put her plan in motion immediately upon perceiving Acton, but, since she was denied the sight of him throughout that unhappy day, and a certain reluctance prevented her asking Saunders his whereabouts, she was compelled to suffer in silence until the evening. Promptly on the stroke of eight she descended the stairs, a vision in gauze and lace—and found the drawing room empty. Undaunted, she went resolutely on down the hall towards the library, feeling shy but determined. Hesitating only a moment, she opened the door—and stood staring at the unexpected sight that met her eyes.

Acton sat sprawled in the chair behind his desk, the empty decanter at his elbow mute testimony to his condition. But Jessica could not think him in very desperate straits, and remained undismayed. Even now his neck-cloth cascaded from beneath his chin in precise folds of pristine white, every button of his waistcoat remained securely fastened, and if one curling lock had fallen forward on his brow, it but enhanced his already handsome appearance. He blinked at her, and said, "I shall have the devil of a head in the morning."

He spoke with only the faintest slurring of his words, and Jessica, had it not been for the empty bottle, would not have noticed anything amiss with him. More amused than otherwise, she moved forward to take a chair facing him across the desk. "Is is not a rather early hour to be so extremely well to live?" she inquired in demurest accents.

This entirely unexpected reaction to his state of insobriety brought his slightly hazy, but still perfectly knowing, gaze to her face. "I may be somewhat cast away," he retorted, "but not so much so that I don't recognize a cant expression when I hear it. Or do you think I'm drunk?"

"Of course not," she answered sweetly. "Top-heavy, perhaps, but definitely not jug-stung."

He studied her in a detached manner. "My so very ladylike bride," he murmured, while feeling vaguely divorced from his surroundings, and not a little sorry for himself. "My own true love," he said, and, liking the sound of it, repeated it.

She regarded him knowingly. "How like a man," she remarked. "The moment he becomes the least foxed, he needs must berate the first unfortunate female to cross his path."

"My own true love," said his Grace for the third time.

"What am I to do with you?" she asked.

For answer, he rose and made his way around the desk, walking with quite unexceptionable balance, and seized her in a crushing embrace. Jessica, sighing softly, melted against him, her lips soft and yielding beneath the fierceness of his. He raised his head once, to devour her with his eyes, before bending to her

again, his kisses now curiously gentle. Only gradually
did his arms slacken their hold. "I shouldn't have
done that," he said shakily.

"Why not?" she asked him frankly.

"Because I'm drunk."

"Shan't you want to kiss me when you're sober?"

"No," said his Grace, holding to his decision, ham-
mer and tongs.

Jessica was not much perturbed. Never mind whatever he might say, he had just betrayed himself. Smiling at him, she said cheerfully, "And I took such
pains with my appearance. Well, and I won't press
you if you are quite certain you want nothing to do
with me. It does seem a pity, though, I will admit."

He had moved back around to his chair behind
the desk while she spoke, and now sat down. "Under
certain conditions I might very much want more to
do with you, but it has been scarcely any time at
all since you told me I am not to be trusted. Or
have you forgotten?"

"Not at all. It is just that I have this distressing
habit of saying things I do not in the least mean.
But perhaps you have not before known anyone so
muttonheaded?"

"Never in your life have you said anything you did
not mean. So don't try to gull me, my girl, for it
can't be done."

"Then of course I shan't attempt to do so," she
replied, not in the least chastised. "I have been meaning to ask you, Acton," she went on, indicating her
gown. "Do you think this particular shade of blue becomes me?"

"You look beautiful, as you damn well know," he
shot back. "What the devil are you about?"

"Well, if you don't know, I shan't tell you."

There was suddenly an arrested look on his face; he shook his head as if to clear it, and half started up from his chair. She watched hopefully—but he sank back down again. "Is this a further attempt to hoax me?" he demanded harshly.

She heaved a disappointed sigh. "There is only one thing to be done," she said, and crossed to the bell cord. "I daresay we cannot carry on a sensible conversation until you are somewhat restored."

"Oh, can't we? Well, let me tell you—"

"You have been doing so since I entered the room. Don't think that I am shocked, for I'm not. No, not a bit of it. But I think we will do better to wait until you have your restorative. Ah, yes, Saunders," she said to the butler answering her ring. "Please bring a pot of strong tea."

Saunders cast a glance at Acton. "May I suggest the addition of sugar, your Grace?" he said to Jessica. "I understand it to have beneficial properties."

"No!" interjected Acton. "Bring a bottle of brandy."

"A pot of strong tea, thank you, Saunders," confirmed Jessica, returning to her seat.

Acton bestowed one devastating glance on her. "You have a knack for getting your own way, haven't you?"

"I do my poor best," she replied. "Oh, Acton! What can have possessed you to drink in this imprudent fashion? For you surely have had too much, you know."

"What possessed me!" he repeated, incredulous. "My God! First we are besieged by a pack of unwanted guests, and then the minute I get you alone, you suggest I set out in pursuit of Lady Stanley. Hotfoot, you said."

"You were sensible not to have done so. You really didn't care to, did you? I must own I realized that only after I had thought about it. Well, here comes Saunders. I hope you will drink the tea without a fuss."

He smiled, though with an effort. "It seems I must if I am to have any peace."

Jessica had expected him to be more difficult, and so was relieved. Saunders, however, shared no such feeling, and glanced anxiously at his employer as he carefully placed the silver tray upon the desk. He had arranged it with care, but ruefully admitted to himself that the nicety of the appointments did little to disguise the contents of the pot.

Acton looked first at one of them and then at the other. "That will be all," he told Saunders with dangerous restraint.

The butler bowed and removed himself from the room, relieved not to have the teapot hurled at his head, while regretting not being present to see his Grace down its contents.

Jessica smiled at Acton. "I hope I haven't also fallen under your displeasure," she remarked agreeably. "I don't scruple to own I shouldn't care to find myself on the wrong foot again."

"You don't suffer from any qualms of conscience that I can see," he retorted, resolutely pouring out a cup and raising it to his lips. Lowering it, he eyed her balefully. "Either I'm mistaken," he said, "or you're the most precious vixen to ever cross my path."

"Is it that bad?"

"Whatever could Saunders have put in it?"

"Sugar," Jessica laughed. "Quite a cupful, I shouldn't wonder."

This remark had the desired effect. Acton was around his desk in three long strides. Swept up into his arms, Jessica returned his kisses with an ardor to match his own. "You do love me," he murmured against her lips. "You do!"

Raising her head, she gazed somewhat breathlessly into his eyes. "Oh, Acton," she chided him. "You know I do."

He gave a shout of ecstatic laughter and kissed her again, his arms tightening until she could scarcely breathe. "I will make you happy," he promised. "I vow I will."

She smiled lovingly at him, not even having to pretend for the sake of her plan, and tenderly smoothed the errant lock of hair from his brow. "I have been wanting to do that since I first entered the room," she admitted softly.

"Why didn't you?"

"I could never have been so bold. But never mind. I daresay I will learn."

His hands slid downwards to her waist. "There is much you will learn," he grinned, an unmistakable glint in his eye. "And though your gown is becoming," he added mischievously, "I have a strong desire to see you without it."

Sounds of a disturbance in the hall brought his head around. "Damnation," he muttered under his breath, releasing Jessica as footsteps approached the library door. Two unhappy individuals, ushered into the room by an extremely reluctant Saunders, seemed acutely aware of the butler's disapproval, and stood looking helplessly at the Duke. One of them wore the uniform of a constable, while to even the most inexperienced eye the other was easily identified as a police inspector. Swallowing his irritation, Acton said, "Well, gentlemen?"

The Inspector shifted his feet uneasily, his eyes wavering back and forth between the countenances of their Graces until he seemed to goggle. He felt the unluckiest man alive. Rogues and cutthroats he could deal with, but the aristocrat before him now was a powerful and wealthy lord. He shifted his feet again, and said in an apologetic voice, "We are sorry to disturb you, your Grace, but the evidence—that is—"

Acton's brows shot up. "Evidence?" he said. "Of what?"

"Murder, your Grace." The Inspector licked dry lips. "Of Lady Imogene Stanley and one Froggie Dupree."

Acton's eyes grew larger as he stared at the embarrassed minion of the law, his face expressing no definite reaction. "What?" he asked, finally. "And what has that to do with me?"

"If it pleases your Grace, a witness swears you were present—"

This extremely unexpected statement might well have daunted a gentleman of lesser stature than a Duke, but Acton remained unmoved. "I do not doubt you believe your information to be correct, but you are in error. Shall we take a seat while you tell me what the devil this is about?"

The Constable, casting a worried look around, followed the Inspector to the sofa, but unlike his superior who was striving to attain some slight mastery of the moment, he refused all offers of refreshment and perched on the edge of his seat, thinking it only a matter of time before he would be called upon to grapple with the crisis. At the time he had answered the summons to the Hare and Hounds, he had been seized with a vague sense of misgiving. Instinct told him the landlord had been lying.

The Inspector, meanwhile, speaking in tones of

growing authority, regaled his Grace with, in the Constable's opinion, a thoroughly garbled rendition of events. It was the gentleman who had been shot; her ladyship had had the life choked out of her, and a nasty business it had been all around. But it was the Inspector's unveiling of his theory that the fated couple had been apprehended in the process of an elopement that fairly put his teeth on edge. Her ladyship had already had a husband, as his superior should have known, and one need only glance at her Grace to see the foolishness of thinking his Grace's eye might wander.

The effect of his elocution upon the Duke was not quite what the Inspector hoped for. His Grace threw back his head and laughed. "I see you weren't acquainted with Lady Stanley," he said.

This was too much for the Inspector. Any dreams he might have had of personal glory were beginning to evaporate, along with his theories on the case. "I fail to see what bearing that can have on the case," he said somewhat testily.

"She would never relinquish her title to marry any man, unless of course by so doing she would acquire one of higher rank. You will need to look farther afield for your rogue than a rejected suitor, Inspector. And there is a Lord Stanley, you know."

The Inspector fixed him with a jaundiced eye. "Have you forgotten the witness, your Grace?" he asked with a gleam of triumph in his expression.

"I wouldn't base my conjecture on that, if I were you," Acton advised him imperturbably. "As I told you before, I am not your man. To my knowledge I've never been near the—Hare and Hounds, I believe you said?"

The interview seemed fraught not only with a lack, in the Inspector's mind, of cooperation, but with an entirely unforeseen absence, again in the Inspector's opinion, of dignity. Feeling the heady weight of authority, he inadvisedly said in tones of approaching doom, "May I inquire after your Grace's movements during the early hours of last evening?"

"You may not!" immediately came Acton's cold reply.

A glimpse of his outthrust jaw was enough to give Jessica a very good notion of the state of his temper. The blame, after all, sat astride her own shoulders. Had she not quarreled with him, he would have been in her own company. Into the silence, she spoke. "His Grace was with me, Inspector," she said quite distinctly, and with finality.

An explosive: "No!" burst from Acton's lips. A scowl now darkened his countenance, but he spoke in altered tones. "Her Grace mistakes the date, Inspector. Last evening I rode out over the estate. Alone."

"Alone, your Grace?" repeated the Inspector, a faint note of suspicion creeping into the query. "At night?"

"Alone," reaffirmed Acton. "And now, before this interview proceeds further, I will ask you to excuse her Grace. It is not, I am sure you will agree, a discussion fit for female ears."

He had crossed to the door while he spoke, and now stood waiting for Jessica to depart the room. She did not want to leave, and stood by her chair looking imploringly at him, one hand pressed to her breast distractedly. A number of objections ran through her mind, but she already knew the expression on his face well enough not to persist. Seeing nothing for it but to obey, she moved forward, then paused on the threshold and hesitantly put out her hand. His hand closed on hers as he smiled reassuringly. "I will be up shortly," he said, and quietly closed the door.

Jessica went upstairs feeling considerably put out. That the Inspector should dare to harbour the notion, much less presume to suggest, that Acton could be involved in heinous crime she found intolerable. Equally unacceptable was any possibility that he might suspect she herself could question his innocence. With this in mind, she searched her brain for some means of demonstrating her affection. It did not take her long to hit upon the very thing.

Selecting a diaphanous gauze nightdress, she allowed her maid to help her don the delectably filmy concoction, and stood back to study the effect. If that did not arouse Acton, she thought with a little smile, nothing could. Next she sat herself down at her dressing table and had Agnes brush her hair until it shone. "Leave it loose," she said, gazing dreamily at her image reflected in the mirror. If the sight of glistening tresses flowing freely over bare shoulders did not put Acton in a fair way to admitting defeat, it would be a pity.

Turning in her chair, she pursed her lips as she looked around the room, her gaze coming at last to rest upon the bed. The covers, demurely turned down in readiness for her occupancy, caught her eye. She flew across the room to lay them back on the other side as well. Studying the scene through narrowed lids, she nodded to herself and set about the task of extinguishing the candles, leaving one glowing on the table beside the bed. Satisfied, she took a last critical look at her reflection and sank down onto a chair to await developments. She had only the sketchiest knowledge of what would soon take place in the large four-poster, but after the pleasure of Acton's kisses she was all agog to find out.

She hadn't long to wait. Hearing Acton's step in her sitting room, she crossed to the door and stood framed by the dark wood, the light behind her revealing her body completely, as she had known it would. She might as well have been unclothed, for the gauze of her gown concealed little from his view.

He stood stock still and stared, his eyes feasting on pink-tipped breasts, the small nipples pertly thrusting from their glowing mounds. "God!" he groaned and seized her. Kissing her frantically, he held her tighter and tighter in his arms, moulded her body to his; dropping his hands to her hips, he pressed his hardness against her softness, ground his manhood against her thighs.

Jessica was momentarily shocked. Never had he touched her so before. But strange ripples were coursing through her body, sensations such as she had never known were taking command of her senses. Flinging her arms about his neck, she pushed her body closer to his, returning his kisses, until, finally, he swept her off her feet and carried her to the large bed waiting in the softly glowing candlelight.

Acton awakened early the following morning and lay contentedly gazing at Jessica cuddled close against his chest. Leaves fluttering beyond the windows dappled the sunlight that shone upon her breasts, forming and reforming soft shadows. He lay watching in fascination for a time, before reaching out a hand to alter the shapes of shadows with the movement of his fingers. Chuckling in delight, he continued with his play until a stirring in his loins led his thoughts to the sweet warmth of her. "Jessica," he whispered, gently flicking a nipple with his finger. "Jessica," he insisted, teasing it until her eyes flew wide.

Startled, she lay gazing up at him, flushing slightly at the fire kindling in his eyes. "G-good m-morning," she stammered, and flushed more rosily still to feel his hands lightly on her skin. "Shall you wish your ch-chocolate now?" she managed, reaching for the pull beside the bed.

"Don't be a goose," he laughed, pulling her back into his arms. "I have other fare in mind."

Much later she stirred in his embrace and rubbed her cheek against his chest, enjoying the firm feel of him. "Acton," she murmured low. "Are we having a—well, a debauchery?"

"We are having a splendid one, my love. Are you enjoying it?"

"Yes, I am," she smiled, going off on a trill of laughter. "I'm enjoying it very much indeed."

CHAPTER VI

The sights and impressions of her first tour of Aynesworth left Jessica with her brain in a whirl. On a rainy afternoon immediately following luncheon, she went with Acton along its corridors and through its many rooms, its treasures unfolding before her wondering eyes. She tried to absorb it all, and asked a hundred questions, for she would have liked above all things to picture him growing up amid such surroundings. It was indeed a great house. Admirable in every respect, its salons were elegant, its pictures masterpieces of the first quality. By the time they had traversed the ground floor, Jessica was feeling very much out of her depth. He gave no sign of having noticed, but a silence she made no effort to break soon fell, and while she was trying to think of something to say, Acton, with what she assumed to be instinctive consideration, brought the tour to an end.

It was at breakfast a fortnight later that he announced his intention of journeying to London. He spoke lightly but a certain note in his voice revealed his regret. "A hearing concerning the murders is in progress, and I intend to confront the landlord of the Hare and Hounds in person."

Jessica was immediately intrigued, of course, but Acton refused quite firmly to allow her to accompany him. A spirited argument ensued over his decision, but he ended it by saying pleasantly that it was not a fit affair for her to become involved in, and, regardless of any further reasoning she was able to bring forth, remained adamant.

So it was that two mornings later Jessica found herself riding out alone, and not much enjoying it. Entering the woods with Jenks trailing a discreet distance behind, she suddenly experienced a feeling of unease. A nervous tremor rippling down her spine, she peered around in the gloom, but could discern nothing of an unusual nature.

"What is it, your Grace?" Jenks asked anxiously, moving his mount closer than was his custom.

"I had the oddest feeling we were being watched."

Glancing at her questioningly, he quickly averted his eyes. "I see no one, your Grace," he said hesitantly.

Jessica suddenly felt foolish. With a breeze gently murmuring through the trees, and birds singing from the boughs, the scene could not appear more normal. Jenks must think her behaviour strange. Before she aroused his curiosity further, she turned Lottie about and swiftly rode for home.

Descending the staircase later to partake of the noonday meal, she saw with startled eyes McClean standing in the door of Acton's study, a glass in his hand. "I have been awaiting your company at luncheon," he said unctuously.

"I was not aware you had been invited to visit Aynesworth," she gasped without thinking.

"I do not require an invitation to visit my future home," he replied, laughing jovially. Standing aside with mock courtesy for her to precede him, he added, "Shall we proceed to the dining room, m'dear?"

Luncheon in his company would not be pleasant, she thought as he carelessly dropped into his chair. Spreading his napkin in his lap with a smirk he purred, "I understand you have been ill."

"I cannot imagine where you heard such a thing. As you see, I enjoy excellent health."

"I was informed you imagine a villain lurking behind every tree. You will admit your conduct to be extremely—odd."

"Odd?" Jessica seemed puzzled. "In what way?"

"Come, come, m'dear. Considering the singular nature of your attack, it has given me a shock. I do not deny it has given me a shock."

"If you are feeling not quite the thing, McClean, perhaps the comfort of your own home will set you on your feet."

"If I am not enjoying my usual peace of mind, Cousin, it is from worry over you. Since I am Acton's heir, the state of your—emotional well-being must be my first concern." When she would have interrupted, he held up one white hand. "We will have my doctor in. He will advise us as to the suitability, nay, the necessity, of confining you to your rooms, that you should not harm yourself—you understand."

"I understand only this," she said, rising to her feet. "You will pack your bags and leave. At once. See to it, Saunders," she added to the butler as she passed from the room. Ten minutes later she was strolling in the gardens thinking of Acton, yearning for his return, and quite unconscious of the blossom she was shredding with her fingers.

* * *

Six more days were to pass, however, before she heard from him. Recognizing his hand on the note arriving with her morning chocolate, she eagerly broke the seal, spread the sheet, and read:

> October 4th
>
> I have dispatched instructions to Saunders to send you up to London. I will expect your arrival by tomorrow evening at the latest.
>
> Yours, Acton.

Jessica stared at the missile in disbelief, a frown darkening her face. Gone these many days, she thought, and he sends this! An odiously brief letter without one word of love! Springing up from her bed, she balled the note into a wad, and flung it on the floor. Agnes, conversant with Saunders' instructions, for the household had been turned topsy-turvy since word arrived at dawn, hesitantly said, "Shall I pack, your Grace?"

"Oh!" stormed Jessica furiously. "He is the most hateful wretch alive."

It was fast approaching the hour of six o'clock when Jessica's equipage drew up before Acton House in St. James's Square. Four stories tall, and built of a whitish stone, the residence boasted one of the most imposing porticos to be found in town. By the time a footman had opened the massive mahogany door, a groom had sprung down to assist her to alight.

To say that she crossed the portal with a sprightly step would be far wide of the mark. For Jessica, still very much incensed with Acton, requested his Grace be informed of her arrival, bespoke tea in her rooms, and immediately went upstairs. She was just in the process of removing her bonnet when the door opened, and Acton came in.

"I trust you had a pleasant journey," he said politely.

She turned slowly and regarded him somewhat witheringly from across the room. "You don't sound as though you were glad to see me," she remarked, drawing off her gloves.

"But of course I am, my dear," he said lightly, yet with a restraint in his voice she could not miss.

She came slowly forward, trying to read the expression on his face. "I should have thought to have heard from you. If I have displeased you in some way, I beg your pardon."

"You have not displeased me in any way at all, Jessica. How could you? Have you no idea how much I love you?" He turned abruptly away. "Something unforeseen has occurred which makes it impossible for us to continue in our marriage as before. There has been much in my life which I deplore, but I am not so depraved as to harm you."

"How could you possibly do that? It is a great piece of impertinence on your part—"

"You don't understand," he interrupted, his voice harsh. "I came to London with the express intention of putting a period once and for all to any question concerning my innocence. But I met with the intelligence that my coach was seen the evening of the murders drawn up before the Hare and Hounds. So far as I can discover, several witnesses will attest to it. Yes, you may well stare, my dear."

"Well, I must say I hope you credit me with too much sense to refine on that! Any testimony given by patrons of a—a low haunt can hardly be considered at all. Surely the authorities will place scant reliance on anything they might choose to say."

"But the witnesses were not patrons of the Hare and Hounds, my dear. They are quite respectable yoemen who just happened to be passing by. I cannot make head or tail of it, but they are standing pat on what they claim they saw."

"And what of McCauley? Surely the authorities have questioned your own coachman?"

"He has told them I was nowhere near the place that evening. But do not base your hopes on that. McCauley is a servant in my employ, remember. His testimony must be considered biased, if not downright false."

"But the thing is, Acton, you and I both know it isn't. I don't mean to be one of those pushy females who must have her say, so I won't tease you with protestations I know you do not wish to hear. But if it is not too distasteful to you, I should like to know what all of this has to do with our marriage."

He did not speak for a moment, but looked steadily at her, his face grim. "You are not so green as to fail to realize the natural result of our continuing as before. I am not so mindless of all that is proper as to get you with child."

There was a little less colour now in her cheeks, but she said steadily enough, "Must you insult me? Nothing could give me greater joy than to bear your son."

"My God!" he exclaimed, the words wrenched from his throat. "Do you imagine I don't want it? I want it above all else, but every consideration of honour forbids me to take advantage of your innocence. You cannot know what it would mean to a child, growing up under a cloud on his father's name. Not to mention the impropriety of thrusting myself on you," he added bitterly.

"If that is all that is troubling you, put it from your mind. I am sensible of the odd notions you sometimes take into your head, but I never would have expected you to concoct anything so idiotic as this. You may propose to deny your own pleasure, sir, but I do not intend you should deny me mine."

"Jessica," he began, and checked himself. After a tiny pause, he sighed, and said, "Perhaps it would be better had we never married."

"Perhaps it would," she agreed, stung. "I don't wonder that you should find me much beneath your touch. For a duke of the realm to have allied himself with a girl won at gaming—"

He was upon her in two strides. "How dare you!" he demanded, shaking her furiously. "If you ever say such a thing again—"

"What am I to believe?" she asked the moment he released her. "Oh, I know you think to bamboozle me with a tale even a ninnyhammer could not swallow, but I am not so unknowing as all that. Anyone could only suppose you have t-tired of me," she finished on a sob.

"Tired of you!" he exploded incredulously, a muscle jerking in his cheek. "There is nothing I'd like better right this minute than to—" He half reached for her, but recollecting himself, dropped his arms. "You will accept my decision," he said gently, crossing the room to stand beside the door. "I think you will find life in the metropolis enjoyable, Jessica. You need only tell me which entertainments you wish to attend. London may be rather thin of company this early in the season, but enough of the ton will have returned by now to make up a party for any amusements you might desire. My dear, you will find it is for the best. When my name is cleared—"

"I simply cannot believe this is happening," she broke in, her eyes fixed on his face in an imploring way.

"I love you, Jessica. It is because I do that I have resolved not to hurt you. You must try to understand, and to help me, for I cannot live apart from you."

Mutely nodding, Jessica dropped her eyes, and so did not see the pain in his own eyes, nor the droop of his shoulders as he left the room and quietly closed the door. She sat where he had left her, not so much folding her hands in her lap as gripping them tightly together. Very well then, my lord Duke, she thought. We will go along with your absurd notions for the present, but eventually someone else will have her say.

Acton, she soon found, was as good as his word. Nothing could have exceeded his intentions, nor the promptitude with which he escorted her about the town. In every respect he stood ready to oblige her, and went with her to Westminster Abbey and the Tower of London; and if he viewed with reluctance the prospect of a boat trip on the Thames, he did not allow it to show on his face. She enjoyed these excursions—it would have been impossible for her not to have been diverted—and on the whole they dealt agreeably enough together. It was only when she was not with him that despair would overtake her, plunging her into such a state of anguish she would find maintaining a pleasant mien almost beyond her powers. Fortunately for Acton, the *haut ton* came flooding back to London before the novelty of such pleasures could pall, and gilt-edged invitation cards began arriving in large numbers at the mansion in St. James's

Square. Jessica's spirits so rose in fact, at attending routs and balls and all of the other forms of entertainment with which society amused itself, that she was soon able to banish for short periods of time her feelings of despair.

But if the appearance upon the social scene of her Grace of Acton met with hearty approval from a majority of its members, in one quarter, at least, it failed to do so.

Lady Eurice Alastair, ushered into the blue salon of the Dowager Duchess's house in Cavendish Square, settled herself comfortably in an elegant little French *fauteuil,* recruited her energies with tea and biscuits, and delivered a somewhat disjointed recitation of Jessica's excesses. "Depend upon it," she finished in failing accents. "She has conducted herself in a most encroaching way."

"I had heard," said Grandmama, sitting very straight in her chair, "that she has become quite the rage."

Under her sister-in-law's stern gaze, Lady Eurice fidgeted with the strings of the bonnet tied beneath her chin. "I am sure you must be pleased, as indeed I am, if she has become a toast. But her shocking behaviour, my dear! I am bound to say I cannot approve the bestowing of a token upon Lord Ames. I have it on best authority that she brazenly tucked her handkerchief—and with her initials embroidered on it, too —smack into his lordship's pocket. I don't wonder it should cause talk, for they were right out on the dance floor at the time where anyone could see."

"Did Acton raise any objection?"

"Well, as to that, no. But you know how he is, Clementine. He just laughed, and clapped his lordship on the back."

"I would say he displayed a deal of sense. If that is

all you have to relate of Jessica's behavior, Eurice, I think you have scant cause for concern."

"Oh, but it isn't, I assure you," Lady Eurice hastened to say. "I must label it shocking, though I'm sure her madcap ways may not seem so to you, for her to have been seen driving Acton's phaeton—and the high-perch one at that—through Hyde Park. And I must say, she could have picked a time other than between five and six when she was bound to be observed by the most elevated members of the ton."

"I must confess you have at last succeeded in surprising me, Eurice. How many horses were pulling the contraption?"

"Well, I couldn't say, though I do suppose Acton would have taken the ribbons were she in danger of oversetting them. I understand he found the exploit vastly diverting, but then he is not in a position to censure his wife in public."

Grandmama thought of replying with a great deal of asperity, but at that moment Acton's footsteps sounded in the hall, and the door opened to admit him. He gave no sign of surprise at finding his greataunt present, but came across the room to salute her hand. "I trust I have not arrived at an inopportune time?" he said pleasantly.

"Yes. Well, n-no. That is, I only called—"

"—to lament my shortcomings, as usual, I infer," said his Grace languidly.

"I declare you are becoming as disdainful as your father!" snapped Lady Eurice. She arose with an angry flounce, twitched her skirts in place, announced it was time for her to leave, and, refusing Acton's offer to escort her to her carriage, marched stiffly through the door.

"I gathered from Eurice's somewhat incoherent discourse that you and Jessica have been setting the town by its heels," said Grandmama.

Acton, who was in the act of helping himself to a generous selection of little sweet biscuits, said absently, "I know. But we've done nothing of note, I assure you."

"What are you doing in town in the first place?" asked Grandmama candidly. "I should think you would wish to have Jessica to yourself."

"I need hardly remind you, ma'am, of my dislike of answering questions."

"Well, if you wish to know what I think—though I make no doubt you don't—you would do well to control Jessica. Don't misunderstand me, boy. I have no fault to find. But you know as well as I how quickly one can become persona non grata, should one overstep the mark."

"I hope I have sufficient experience to prevent that from occurring," said his lordship calmly.

At about the same moment his Grace was speaking so complacently, Jessica was upstairs in the house in St. James's Square, staring at the door between their bedrooms, a look of loathing upon her face. That Acton should dare to suppose it would remain closed was ludicrous in the extreme. She only needed some means to rouse him, she thought, and sought in her mind for a scheme to make him jealous.

CHAPTER VII

Contrary to Lady Eurice's expectations, Jessica's exploits failed to bring her into bad favour with the ton. Quite the reverse. If her Grace of Acton was not present, no soirée could be termed select, no rout or ball a squeeze. Jessica was perfectly ready to be amused, and to a certain extent she was, but under her enjoyment lurked a dull ache of longing, never quite forgotten and sometimes acute, for she was under no illusion where Acton was concerned. In his own way he remained determined in his purpose and, seeming little moved by anything she chose to do, turned a blind eye to the most affecting gyration she was able to contrive. While she might conceivably feel some doubt of the eventual success of her plans— and even she must concede in her own mind the possibility of failure, for her notions of propriety forbade her doing anything too terribly outrageous—she nevertheless remained confident.

Acton would have been quite singular had he failed to appreciate the humour of it all. Despite a marked disinclination to put himself to the trouble of monitoring Jessica's flights, he knew of them, for she was nothing if not open in everything she did. Had her starts reached lamentable proportions, he would, of course, have bestirred himself, but as it was he was perfectly content to let matters drift.

Not so Jessica. Entering his study one fine morning, she took a deep breath and crossed to the chair beside his desk. "Before you say anything, Acton, I should tell you I have done something dreadful. I expect you will be furious," she finished in a rush.

"Then perhaps you had better tell me about it," he murmured, resuming his seat.

She began nervously to pleat the silk of her skirt. "I couldn't resist it, you see," she offered breathlessly, raising her eyes to peep at him. "It has the most dashing yellow wheels, and there can be nothing more wonderful than its body. It is shining black, you know."

A hint of surprise flickered across his face. "I have long been prepared for the worst, my dear," he said softly, "but I have the most lowering thought that you are speaking of a conveyance of some sort."

"Well, I—yes, Acton. I am."

"Ah," sighed his lordship. "That, of course, makes the matter abundantly clear."

"It is a curricle, you will understand," Jessica said, with a certain defiance in her tone.

"I believe I need not ask," murmured his lordship. "You have purchased a curricle."

She looked at him appealingly. "You will let me keep it, will you not? I like it excessively, Acton, and well—just think of the dash I will cut, in tooling it about."

His lordship found himself putty in the hands of

his beloved. Smiling inwardly upon his defeat, he said, "May I inquire when it is to be delivered from the coachmaker's?"

Jessica gave a gasp. "Next week," she said, her face brightening. "Oh, Acton!"

There came a pause. His lordship, a smile lurking in his eyes, said, finally, "You will forgive me, my dear, but I have one further question. Have you purchased the horses?"

Jessica stared at him, dumbfounded. "Horses?" she repeated numbly.

"I believe they customarily pull a curricle."

"Yes, of course," she nodded, flushing. "How foolish of me."

"If you wish it, my dear, I will send Jenks to purchase a pair."

"You will?" she said thankfully. "I must own I shouldn't know how to go about it."

"Then I trust we can consider the matter settled." Seeing the expression on her face, he added, pensively, "Or can we?"

Jessica drew a deep breath. "There is one thing more," she said with difficulty. "I would very much like a little liveried servant—a tiger."

The silence seemed to her to drag while he studied her. "I must admit," he said, finally, "the thought had not occurred to me."

"You will consider it, will you not?" she asked, smiling upon him entrancingly. "I would like it above all things, and no other lady has a tiger."

"Then, by all means," he said somewhat dryly. "I need not ask, of course, whether you have already selected him."

Jessica flashed a smile at her husband. "He is the most adorable little black boy," she said, laughing.

"Just think of the sensation, Acton, when we first appear in public."

"Alas," he said. "I am thinking of it."

"You mean," she said, digesting this, "it would cause a scandal? For if it will, I won't do it," she added heroically.

"I trust your credit as the Duchess of Acton will see you through," he answered truthfully. "I was thinking of something else entirely."

"You mean—Acton, you cannot mean that people would look askance at you!"

He glanced at her. "I do not intend telling you what I mean," he said deliberately.

"Why?" Jessica demanded somewhat truculently.

"Nothing is ever gained by raking over the past."

"Indeed?" she said tartly. "Then you have something to hide?"

He fished his snuffbox from a pocket and flicked it open. "I very much fear that I have, my dear," he remarked, taking a pinch.

"Is that all you are going to say?" Jessica cried, her lip trembling. "For if it is, I will tell you I think you horrid!"

His lordship returned the snuffbox to his pocket. "Shall we leave it at that, my dear?" he said, then stood by, helplessly watching her flounce from the room.

Jessica played back this scene in her mind for days, wondering what course of action she should take. But as she went about the business of acquiring her tiger and outfitting him, and with thoughts of revenge spinning in her pretty head, she seemed incapable of formulating a plan sufficiently annoying to startle Acton. The tiger himself unknowingly provided her with just the thing she sought. Grinning broadly from pride in his little satin suit, he bowed before her, salaaming for all the world like a pint-sized Indian potentate.

Three days later she drove forth, at the fashionable hour of promenade, to startle not only Acton but society as well. The curricle in itself would have created a stir, but it was the tiger, in all truth, who drew the attention of passersby. Perched up on his seat at the rear of the curricle, his little face solemn under a yellow turban with a feather plume, he sat with arms folded across his bare chest, and resisted the temptation to gaze down upon his person. He was pleased with the sleeveless jacket and matching yellow slippers with their upcurling toes, but it was the trousers he gloried in. Full of leg and caught in tight about the ankle, the red satin glowing in the sunlight brought him his greatest joy.

It was by the best of good fortune that one of the first to witness their progress should be Acton. He had halted beside Lady Langdon's landaulet to exchange a few words with her, and caught sight of Jessica before she saw him. A look of surprise flickering across his face, he murmured his farewells to her ladyship and urged Beelzebub forward. In a moment the curricle had pulled up beside him, and his by now amused gaze was sweeping over the tiger. "Please accept my felicitations," he sail, bowing slightly. "You have outdone yourself, my dear."

"I thought you would appreciate it."

"I'm sure you did," he returned, moving Beelzebub back. "Drive on, my dear. Your audience awaits."

Jessica's new turnout did occasion chatter among the ton, but it wasn't long before her latest idiosyncracy stopped raising eyebrows. What would have been impossible to a lady of less notable stature proved

quite allowable to her Grace of Acton. Well enough
pleased, she saw no better course open to her than to
cast around for another peccadillo to entertain her
lord.

Never one to neglect an opportunity, Jessica, on the
occasion of Lady Colson's card party, took it into her
head to face Acton across a gaming table. It fell to
Lord Lester, who quite by accident had had the good
fortune to lead her into the last set, to stroll with her
through the various rooms in search of his Grace.

"Are you sure you wouldn't rather return to the
dance?" he finally screwed up the courage to suggest.
"It isn't at all the thing, you know, to seek the company of your husband. You should avoid Acton like
the plague."

"Yes, I know it isn't very fashionable," she answered.
"But I'm afraid I seldom do what I ought."

"I'm sure that whatever you do, you do it charmingly," he replied in his most gallant manner, standing aside at the entrance to the green salon for her to
precede him.

Four tables had been set up in the room, each large
enough to accommodate six persons. Flunkies moved
among them bearing trays of wine to players intent on
the roll of dice or the turn of a card, while others of
the company stood about exchanging pleasantries with
friends and observing the play. Jessica spied Acton at
the fifty-guinea table and moved forward in a swish
of silk. "I've come to take a hand," she said, smiling
upon him swimmingly.

He looked up in faint surprise, and rose to his feet.
"But of course, my dear," he said, pulling back his
chair preparatory to seating her in it. "I was not aware
that you are fond of pharaoh."

"Well, as to that, I'm not as a rule. But I must not

take your place," she added, realizing every chair about
the table was taken.

"You are welcome to my seat," Lord Ames said.
"Acton has the devil's own luck. My pockets are to
let."

"You will stake me, Acton, will you not?" Jessica
asked, taking the place between Lord Benchley and a
Mr. Wardly, newly come to town.

Acton placed a stack of chips before her. He was
to place many such stacks before her as the evening
wore on, for Jessica, though she was not enjoying the
role she had chosen, played with reckless abandon,
chatting gaily the while. The sums she was losing so
cheerfully did not trouble her in the least, for she
remained unaware of their total. Acton's unmoved
countenance consumed her every thought. He did not
appear to be in an unhappy mood, and drank every
glass of Burgundy placed before him by a flunkey; to
remarks addressed to him, he answered briefly, lapsing
into silence the moment the words had been exchanged. A jest by Lord Ames roused him momentarily, and drew a perfunctory smile to his lips, but beyond that he remained abstracted. Young Mr. Wardly,
unacquainted with his Grace, and therefore thinking
his conduct unexceptional, remained unaware that
anything could be amiss. His only concern, if indeed
he dared be concerned, lay in the sums her Grace was
wagering. For Mr. Wardly, himself the principal ben-
eficiary of her careless play, found himself embarrassed by his own wholly unexpected good fortune. It
could not be deemed seemly, in his opinion, to win so
much from a lady. He stood it as long as he could, and
said, finally, appalled by his own temerity, "Should we
not lower the stakes?"

Acton glanced up at him. "My dear Wardly," he

said pleasantly. "I'm sure we have no fault to find with your run of good fortune."

"But it hardly seems sporting—I mean, to win from a lady—"

His Grace ignored the flush spreading across the youthful face opposite to him. "Her Grace has no objection," he murmured, while not permitting his gaze to wander from Mr. Wardly's eyes to his flushed cheeks. "Nor have I, I might add."

"I don't know what I ought to do," Mr. Wardly admitted miserably. "It isn't as though I needed the money—"

"Acton doesn't either, dear boy. Don't put yourself into a pucker," Lord Benchley said, picking up his cards. "Shall we resume play? I have great expectations for this hand."

"You do?" Jessica asked. "I can't say I care for mine."

"Now that, my dear Lady Alastair, you should never say, much less think," Lord Benchley gently reproved. "Keep your opponents guessing, that's the ticket."

"Really?" Jessica said delightedly. "And I thought I was being quite clever. Am I truly so transparent?"

"But charmingly so," returned his lordship gallantly.

"I wish I might believe you are right," sighed Jessica. "I own I was dismayed to lose that last hand, but I suppose I knew I would from the outset. It is my headache, I don't doubt."

"Why did you not say so?" Acton asked, rising, a crease appearing between his brows. "Come. I will conduct you home."

"Will you, indeed? I would as lief you did, if you don't mind."

Acton took her hand and drew it through his arm. Jessica sketched a curtsy to the gentlemen on their feet about the table, and smiled upon Mr. Wardly. "Perhaps we will play again," she said pleasantly, and, moving away, left with Acton.

It was past two o'clock when they arrived home in St. James's Square. Jessica, yawning slightly, crossed the hall towards the stairs. "If it wouldn't inconvenience you, my dear," Acton's voice spoke at her elbow, "I would like a moment of your time."

"Now?" she said. "I'm going to bed."

"I will be brief," he insisted, holding open the door into his study.

"But I have the headache."

He looked steadily at her, his look of gravity giving way to one of amusement. "Have you, Jessica? I think not."

"Oh!" she stormed, and stamped her foot. "Of all the—the disobliging—"

"Pray do not offer me compliments I do not deserve," he said calmly. "Shall I carry you?"

Jessica shot him a speculative glance, then crossed the hall and went into the room. "You are full of threats," she said with what semblance of indifference she could muster. "What did you wish to talk about?"

"Nothing important enough to cause you to fire up at me," he replied pleasantly. "I hope I am able to afford your excesses, my dear, but you were a trifle extravagant tonight, you will agree."

"I haven't the least doubt you think so, but it was vastly diverting, Acton."

"I am happy you enjoyed yourself, of course," he murmured noncommittally. "Jessica, have you any idea of the sum you lost?"

"I'm afraid not. Was it too terribly much?"

"Some three thousand."

"What!" she shrieked, gazing at him in startled dismay. "I—I couldn't have!"

"Ah, but you did," he said calmly. "You are not to think I mean to ring a peal over your head, for I don't. I perfectly understand you should enjoy yourself."

"Well, but—" Jessica swallowed around the constriction in her throat, and tried to think of something to say.

"There is one thing, my dear. I hope you will not be offended, but do you invariably draw to a trey?"

"That was foolish of me, wasn't it?"

"Very."

"But it would have been so thrilling, had it worked, you know."

"It would indeed," said his Grace.

"I promise not to do it again."

If his Grace found such protestations of future exemplary behaviour amusing, he gave no sign of it. "That is undoubtedly admirable," he said placidly. "My dear, may we agree you will in future stage somewhat less costly exercises for my benefit?"

"Oh!" Jessica gritted through her teeth. "You are odious, sir! Odious, I say!"

"My deplorable disposition is no doubt again at fault," murmured his Grace. "Shall we say I will countenance future escapades, provided they not become too shocking?"

"I imagine I can contrive not to disgrace you," she said, and stalked from the room, closing the door behind her with quite unnecessary force.

Acton, accepting the snub with tolerable equanimity, had no difficulty at all in anticipating future hostile confrontations. Jessica's was hardly the stuff of which cowards are made. There was something in defying him which attracted her, and she was able to devise an unending program of artful schemes designed to spur him into action. To her dismay, he remained unmoved, and seemed to view her most provoking caprices with despicable complaisance. As the days passed she said nothing, but she thought about it often.

Upon the morning following a particularly unnerving defeat at his hands, Jessica sent orders to her groom to bring his Grace's high-perch phaeton around. Having second thoughts, she added a second request for his lordship's greys. No sooner had it arrived before the door than she descended the steps, and allowed the groom to hand her up. Picking up the reins, she dispensed with his services, remaining adamant in the face of his obvious disapproval, and set the horses forward. She met Mr. Wardly at the entrance to Hyde Park and took him up beside her. Refusing his offer to take the ribbons, she drove them on, her air of calm unconcern quite at variance with the quaking of her knees. Surely he must see through her she thought, as she assured him quite falsely that she was used to driving herself about alone. The question of its being Acton's phaeton and not her own curricle, of which she was inordinately proud, she blithely glossed over in her own mind.

"I hadn't realized females could be so resourceful," Mr. Wardly said with no little awe. "I shall not despair of finding a lady who pleases me, in future."

"Have you never clapped eyes on one who did?" she asked, intrigued.

"I did once, ma'am," he admitted. "But nothing came of it. Her Papa wanted me to ride to hounds.

Really, your Grace. What could I do but run for my life?"

"Nothing, I'm sure," Jessica replied, smiling. "I am persuaded any number of young ladies will set their caps for you. You will be thinking of marriage one day soon."

"I'm happy just the way I am. I intend to enjoy town life before I settle down."

They had reached the end of the park by now, and Jessica turned the greys for the return trip. But as she rounded the corner, a sudden gust of wind blew a paper across the horses' path, and before Jessica could think to prevent it the horses bolted. She tugged on the reins in a kind of horrified wonder, all to no avail. The team tore onward at full gallop. To her intense relief, a chestnut head appeared from out of nowhere as Beelzebub crept up alongside the phaeton, then pulled ahead; Acton's hand reached out to grasp the off leader's bridle, checking the pace gradually until they dropped into a canter and finally stopped. Weak with relief, Jessica stared blindly at Acton as he swung down from the saddle and walked back to the phaeton. "If you will be so good as to ride my mount back to Acton House, Mr. Wardly," he said without a trace of emotion in his level voice, "I will drive her Grace home."

Jessica moved over into the space vacated by Mr. Wardly, to allow Acton to settle down beside her, and glanced at him in mute appeal. She didn't need to see the grim set of his lips to realize she had finally gone too far. Nor did the blazing anger she saw in his eyes when his at last met hers do much to alleviate her fears. When they had drawn up before Acton House she allowed him to assist her to the ground, and entered the house, a flush of mortification upon her face. There was nothing for it but to proceed to her rooms and wait.

He came in with an angry stride and stood glaring. "How dared you!" he spat at her. "Your conduct, Madam, passes all bounds!"

Her eyes flashed in return. "How dared I?" she exclaimed, her lips tightening. "How dare you! To speak to me in such a way—"

"I will speak to you any way I damned well please!" he said furiously. "Do you think I will longer tolerate your excesses? Well, I won't!" he fairly shouted, seizing her by the shoulders and shaking her until her hair tumbled loose about her shoulders.

"You are hurting me," she gasped in a quavering voice.

"I will do more than that, Madam, if you ever again make yourself an object of scorn for every gossip to titter about!"

"You are abominable, you—you bully! And quit calling me Madam. I loathe it."

"I have a strong desire to box your ears. Do not press your luck."

"Do not you imagine I'm afraid of you, for I'm not. As for your thinking you can force my obedience by bruising me, I will inform you my flesh will heal, even if your manners won't."

Shocked, his anger evaporated, he stared at the red marks standing out against the whiteness of her skin. "My God, Jessica. I didn't intend—"

"Much you care!"

"I hadn't meant to lose my temper, but you will admit you gave me provocation."

"I do admit it, but you didn't allow me an opportunity to beg your pardon."

"Jessica, after all I have endured, don't tell me you think to put me in the wrong!"

"I wonder if you could be right," she said, much struck. When it appeared he didn't intend saying anything in reply, but merely stood staring at her, she crossed to a chair and sat down. "Well, at least you may console yourself with the thought that I was never so frightened in my life," she admitted ruefully. "I made sure the phaeton would become overset at any moment."

"You could have been killed."

"Yes, I know. I didn't think."

"Jessica, what could have induced you to embark upon such a scheme? You hadn't the strength to control my greys, much less expertise with a high-perch phaeton."

"Good gracious, Acton. I couldn't foresee the outcome," she said, and shot him a mischievous look.

She won no answering smile from him; he was looking worried and rather stern, and after a moment he said, "That's a horrid thought. Are you telling me you mean to judge your behaviour in future by such foolhardy considerations? I should hardly think it possible."

"No, of course not," she said, looking at him somewhat anxiously. "Acton, are you going to—punish me?"

"What a low opinion you must have of me," he said, with a crooked smile. "Have I ever done so?"

"I wouldn't much blame you if you did," she replied, her lip beginning to tremble. "I know you think me horrid—"

"My dear, you are very well aware I think nothing of the kind," he returned placidly. "You will have to forgive me for saying this, Jessica, but you know as well as I that you deliberately set out to vex me."

Jessica flushed. "I seem to have succeeded," she said bluntly. "And I don't care what you say, people won't mind that I drove myself through the park!"

"Certainly not, my dear, in your own curricule, and with your tiger up behind. Any lady of your acquaintance would be in raptures to be in a position to do so."

"Pray, do not be patronizing, Acton," Jessica said stiffly.

"I stand corrected," he answered imperturbably. "I did not intend to annoy you."

Jessica suddenly gave her choke of throaty laughter. "The other ladies are envious, are they not?" she said smugly. "Lady Tweesdale told me just the other day she had teased his lordship to buy her a curricule, but he flatly refused to do so. I must admit," she continued chattily, "it was vastly diverting to have startled society the first time I drove out in mine. You must know, Acton, how I appreciate your having given it to me."

"Since you are pleased, my dear, do you think you could refrain from trying my patience in future?"

"I haven't the smallest doubt I can," she replied blithely, if quite mistakenly.

CHAPTER VIII

For several days following her latest contretemps with Acton, Jessica remained true to her role of decorous wife. Enjoying the advantages of a generous allowance, she beguiled the time in selecting muslins and silks for her dressmaker to sew up for her; she visited the lending library and carried home several volumes, none of which she read; and she attended a ball in the company of Acton. Having determined to abandon any schemes designed to annoy him, she managed to get along quite happily with him, spending several evenings alone with him in perfect accord. Such a state of unrelieved bliss could not, of course, endure.

Having one morning received delivery of a perfectly delectable rose silk gown, Jessica stood before the long mirror in her room, studying the effect. Enthralled, she did not hear the door open, and so had no notion that Acton was in the room until she caught sight of his reflection. Giggling to see him gingerly stepping around the piles of tissue paper littering the floor, she whirled about in an excess of joy. "Isn't it ravishing," she exclaimed, coming to a halt before him. "It's for the ball tonight. I understand there will be fireworks, and dancing on a platform beside the lake." Turning away, she critically viewed her image in the mirror. "Do you know, Acton, I believe I will wear my pearls," she said, her head thoughtfully to one side.

"I hesitate to figure as the serpent in Eden, my dear, but I have been called from town on urgent business. Jules stands ready to escort you to the ball."

"Oh, Acton" she exclaimed, exasperated.

"Don't be cross with me, Jessica. I regret it more than you can know, but Jules's company should not prove too tiresomely monotonous."

And so, perforce, Jessica attended the ball in the company of Lord Ames. She certainly held the eye, with her hair dressed in ringlets rioting about her face. McClean, witnessing her arrival, was hard pressed to conceal his annoyance, and while his eyes rested on her with a malignant expression deep within their depths, he did manage a humourless smile.

It was some time before he approached her. She would have declined his offer to escort her to the refreshment table, but he drew her hand through his arm and led her forward. Short of creating a disturbance, there seemed little she could do, other than to put a smile on her face and go along with him. No sooner had he filled their plates than he fixed her with a mournful eye. "To a person of my sensibilities, the necessity to speak of unpleasant things must necessarily be repugnant. I act only in your best interest, m'dear," he added somewhat hastily.

Jessica's eyes flickered to his face. "If you have something to say, McClean, I wish you would come to the point."

"But such a delicate situation must be handled tenderly, m'dear. I regret bringing grief and embarrassment to so lovely a lady as yourself, but, since I am Acton's heir, the unenviable task of enlightening you has callously descended upon my own unwilling head. For he has abandoned you, you know."

"You have a very poisonous tongue, McClean," she told him patiently. "And your presumptions can only bring you unhappiness. Do bear in mind that Acton is young and vigorous. You can expect him to produce an heir, and you will lose your dubious claim."

He smirked. "To do so requires, shall we say, his attendance upon your person?" he said, tittering.

Jessica gasped, bereft of speech. What a hateful creature he is, she thought, the colour flooding her cheeks. It was quite true his expectations ruled his thinking, but there were limits of conduct beyond which even McClean should not trespass. Eyeing him contemptuously, she said, "I do not wish to appear uncivil, McClean, but I must tell you you will do better to leave your remarks unsaid."

"So you think to blink the facts," he purred, pleased at her discomfiture. "You have been deserted. 'Tis a pity, m'dear, but there it is. Acton now seeks his pleasure away from your side, make no mistake about that. And that brings me to the reason for this little chat. You must flee, m'dear. It isn't as though no one was ever divorced before. Ask anyone here if you don't believe me. They will tell there could be no stigma attached to you for having done so."

"I am out of all patience with you, McClean," she said, rising. "You may as well make up your mind to it. Acton and I are happily married, and will remain so."

The ball had been pleasant for Jessica until now. The dancing beside the lake had been quite gay, with sprightly music, and lantern light reflecting merrily upon the water. But with McClean's hateful remarks it had all gone awry. She continued on through the remainder of the evening, pretending to be in good spirits, but wanting nothing so much as the end of the evening's entertainment. It was really rather difficult to dance and converse agreeably with one's partners when one's heart was not in it. It was enough to give one a headache.

The fireworks display set off following the dancing must be deemed wonderful, but Jessica's mind was taken up in wondering what Acton would have thought of it, and what he was doing, as McClean had remarked, so far from her side.

She awoke early the following morning, after a disturbed night, still thinking of Acton. At once she sighed, and, turning over, tried to go to sleep again. Unable to compose herself, she sat up in bed, her knees drawn up under her chin, and wondered if he too were restless and perhaps thinking of her. Remembering their marriage as it had been before murder intervened to blight it, she thought it impossible that he would not recall with longing the happy times that had meant so much to both of them. This however did not trouble her nearly so much as did thoughts of the future. What troubled her most was the unswerving determination with which Acton stuck to his course. Gentlemen—she had long been made to realize—often took into their heads the most sudden and appalling starts of nonsense, clinging to them tenaciously regardless of how senseless these notions might be. For them, honour was a virtue prized above all else: there was their honour in the name they bore, and honour in the games they played, and honour in the ways in which they dealt with family and friends. Jessica felt obliged to admit she was by now heartily sick of the very word.

The clatter of wheels over the cobbled street outside roused her from these musings. If the milk wagon only now was making its rounds, it could not be past seven of the clock. Agnes, to her relief, put forth no questions at being rung for at such an early hour, but to Jessica's request for Lottie to be brought around, and for her tiger, Agnes replied that her Grace should know it wasn't dignified. She said, excusing her forwardness, that besides its being improper, going about with a little black boy dressed in a heathenish way was like to bring her ladyship nought but grief. Jessica, seeing little connection between the two, trailed across to the wardrobe, to lay a habit upon the bed. Admonishing Agnes to mind her tongue and help her dress, she was soon able to leave her lonely room and descend the stairs. Feeling in no wise buoyed as she usually was by the sight of Will, his small form dwarfed by the size of his horse, she mounted Lottie, and rode off in the direction of Hyde Park.

As she trotted down the Row, Lord Benchley happened to turn his head, and saw them approaching. He wheeled his black to await her arrival; the sight of her enchanted him. In an azure habit with white frogging and lace at her throat, she managed to look fragile yet at the same time capable of controlling her horse. Acton's a lucky devil, he thought, as he doffed his hat. "Never have I been so fortunate in my early morning ride," he said, returning his hat to his head. "I trust I may ride along with you?"

Her brows rose in momentary surprise. "But of course," she said. "I should perhaps inform you I am not in the best of spirits this morning."

"Your company must be thought charming, regardless of your mood," he replied, and laughed. "I hardly need ask if Acton's absence has anything to do with it."

Jessica glanced at him, surprised. It did not seem to her that he was well enough acquainted with her to make such a remark. She could not, however, take exception to his tone. "I will strive to be amusing," she replied, setting Lottie forward. "Tell me, Lord Benchley. Have you known Acton for very long?"

"Our fathers were friends from their days at Oxford together, but mine married some years before Acton's. We would perhaps have become closer companions had we been more of an age." It was some minutes before he spoke again. When he did, it was in the way of an apology. "Forgive me if I sounded impertinent a few moments back," he said with his slow smile. "I did not mean to, believe me."

"You needn't apologize, Lord Benchley. It is refreshing to hear someone speak the truth, for once."

"You are thinking of McClean?" he replied easily. "He seldom says what he means, or means what he says, for that matter."

"Shall we forget him? It is too lovely a day for dreary thoughts."

"It is, at that. But I would like to add one thing more, if I may, Lady Alastair. Should you stand in need of a friend while Acton is away, I hope you will turn to me."

Jessica drew Lottie to a halt, and turned her head to look at him somewhat doubtfully. What he had said came as a complete surprise, though she found no difficulty in interpreting his rather cryptic speech. "That is vastly kind of you, Lord Benchley," she murmured politely. "I trust I will not need to take up your offer."

Nothing further was said on the subject, but she was more likely to find herself in need of assistance during the coming days than she could know. McClean, never one to admit defeat, was busily hatching plans.

At the moment, he was sitting propped up in bed against a bank of pillows, yawning, his nightcap askew atop his head. Disdainfully eyeing the remnants of his breakfast, he picked up the tankard and waived the rest away. "I'm sure I don't know why you haven't thought of something," he told Courtney, taking a long draught of ale. "What d'you think I pay you for?"

"The matter would be more easily resolved, my lord, were her Grace at Aynesworth. In town it becomes rather more difficult."

McClean looked faintly surprised. "I had supposed you a master of intrigue," he said shortly. "Surely you can contrive a time to find one silly female alone!"

"Her Grace attracts attention whenever she appears, my lord. I do not, however, consider the case desperate. If your lordship will but be patient—"

"Damn you!" McClean swore at him. "Acton will return soon. What then, you fool? Tell me that!"

The valet's countenance remained impassive. Courtney's years in service to his lordship had left their mark. He moved a step closer to the bed, and said, in conspiratorial tones, "Upon reflection, I recall her

Grace is often in the company of her tiger, my lord. He always accompanies her when she drives out in her curricle, or goes for a ride in the park. Your lordship may have noticed she seems quite taken with the brat?"

McClean shot a contemplative look at him. "You interest me," he mused thoughtfully, considering the point. "Pray continue."

"I am persuaded her Grace could be made to act rashly, my lord, given the proper inducement. She must surely set out in pursuit, should the tiger come up missing."

"Not bad, Courtney," said McClean, relaxing back against his pillows. "Not bad at all."

"Thank you, my lord. It would perhaps be best, if your lordship concurs, to dispose of the child. Chimney sweeps are ever in need of climbing boys."

"Don't bore me with details," McClean snapped, and drained the tankard. "Now, get out. And don't come back until you have disposed of her Grace."

"May I inquire what your lordship wishes done with the body?"

"What do I care?" shrugged McClean. "Throw it in the Thames."

And so it was that on the following afternoon Jessica sent an urgent note to Lord Benchley at his home in Grosvenor Square. It so happened that his lordship was not at liberty, being in the process of entertaining guests, but he excused himself nevertheless, and went at once to Acton House. Ushered into the small salon, he found Jessica awaiting his arrival, and looking extremely pale. "Do forgive me," she said immediately he entered the room, "but I have received the most distressing news. I really didn't know which way to turn, until I remembered your kind offer of assistance."

"I am happy to be of service," he said calmly, drawing her to the sofa. Seating himself in a chair facing her, he added, "May I inquire what it is that has distressed you?"

"I beg your pardon. How foolish of me. It is my tiger, Lord Benchley. He has been missing since early this morning, and I have just received this," she added, holding out a somewhat crumpled missile. "I cannot understand why anyone should wish to abduct Will."

His lordship raised his brows. "I think there is probably some simple explanation, Lady Jessica. This is undoubtedly someone's idea of a prank. Some people do have an odd sense of humour, you know."

"Oh, do you think so?" she said eagerly. "It is quite true that anyone at all would know how fond I am of Will. But how can he not have returned home by now, Lord Benchley? I can't think an accident has befallen him, for surely I would have been informed."

"Since you haven't heard of an accident, Lady Jessica, shall we assume he hasn't met with one? He has more probably become enchanted with something he found of interest, and has neglected to get in touch with you."

"Perhaps so," she conceded grudgingly. "But that isn't at all like Will."

"If he does not return by tomorrow evening, send me word, and I will see what is to be done. In the meantime, try not to fret."

Lord Benchley shortly took his departure. When he returned home, he found Mr. Wardly awaiting him in the salon, sipping a glass of Madeira. "Still here, Edward?" he said. "Good. I have need of your assistance. Her Grace's tiger has come up missing."

Wardly looked at him over the rim of his wine glass. "You suspect mischief," he said, stating a fact.

"I find myself unable to banish Lord McClean Alastair from my thinking. Her Grace may stand in serious need of protection. I have sent a footman to inform Acton, but until his return we will constitute ourselves her protectors."

The following morning at precisely eleven o'clock, Mr. Wardly called at Acton House to inquire whether there was any news of Will. Upon being informed that there wasn't, he said, "The little blighter needs a caning. If you wish me to administer it, I stand ready to oblige."

"I daresay I shall be too happy to see him to think of punishment," Jessica admitted honestly.

"Don't think me impertinent, but I should not coddle the boy, if I were you. He might enjoy the pampering, and you could end with an imp on your hands."

Jessica chuckled, then turned her head as a footman brought up a note on a silver salver. She pounced on it, her eyes horrified as she read through its few lines. "Oh, no," she gasped, sinking down hard onto a chair. "I simply cannot credit it."

Mr. Wardly crossed to stand before her, frowning. "If I may?" he said briefly, and took the missile from her trembling fingers. Scanning it, he said, "You must not go, of course. The address sounds unsavory to me."

"That cannot signify. I rather fancy that when I arrive, ransom will be demanded."

"You must send for Lord Benchley. He is extremely clever, you know. You must trust him to come up with something."

"How can you suggest such a thing, Mr. Wardly? I must leave at once."

He stared at her, seeming to turn something over in his mind. "Why do you think I called this morning, your Grace? Lord Benchley suspected what might occur, and requested I be present. I am to send for him, which, I must add, is just what I intend to do. I am sorry, ma'am."

His very attitude, though it might infuriate her, had the power of holding her motionless. Dropping her eyes, she mutely nodded, and sat waiting while he left the room to send a footman round to Grosvenor Square. Lord Benchley came at once, and was ushered upstairs to the sitting room where both were awaiting him amid an uncomfortable silence. He wasted no time with formalities. "Mr. Wardly, in the guise of the Duchess of Acton, will keep the appointment," he said. "I trust you have no objection to donning female dress, Edward?"

Jessica, quick of wit, smiled somewhat maliciously upon Mr. Wardly. "You *would* interfere, you know," she said. "Do go along to my dressing room. I am sure Agnes will find just the gown for you."

When the gentlemen later returned to the sitting room, Mr. Wardly, though walking somewhat unsteadily in tight-fitting high-heel shoes, nevertheless presented an altogether acceptable substitute for Jessica. He was wearing a yellow gown, and Agnes had somehow contrived to hide Mr. Wardly's much lighter hair as if it were swept up beneath the high-crown yellow bonnet. He couldn't be better. Jessica collapsed in glee. "If only Acton could see you," she gasped through her laughter.

"He no doubt will," Lord Benchley replied. "I sent word to him last evening. If we had time, we would wait for him. As it is, we had best be off."

It was evident that Jessica would have liked nothing better than to accompany them, but she wished them Godspeed, and sat down to await their return.

She spent a miserable afternoon, rushing to the door each time coach wheels sounded outside in the street, and imagining any number of disastrous conclusions to the drama. The clatter of hooves outside the door at around five o'clock sent her running. "Acton!" she gasped, as he stepped down from his coach. "Oh, Acton," she sobbed, rushing forward to hurl herself into his arms.

"What a pleasant reception," he murmured, holding her close. "I should leave home more often."

"Will is kidnapped, and they have not returned," she said somewhat incoherently. "What can they be doing?"

"Shall we go inside?" he said. "Then you will tell me about it."

"I hardly know what I'm saying," she admitted as she went in with him. "Lord Benchley and Mr. Wardly went to rescue Will. They would not allow me to go, and—"

"Jessica, shall we sit down? You may not wish a glass of wine, but I do," he added, filling two glasses. "Now," he said when she had sipped. "From the beginning."

The worry and anxiety of the past hours came pouring forth as she told her tale. When she had concluded, she felt drained. Smiling wanly, she listened to his matter-of-fact remarks, and felt much better. She had been thinking Will perhaps slain, but with Acton returned, her fears seemed groundless. Fortunately they had only twenty minutes to wait before Lord Benchley and Mr. Wardly were ushered into the room. Jessica gasped to see their appearance. "There was trouble," she said, fear gripping her heart. "Where is Will?"

"Not dead," said Benchley. "I'm glad to see you,

Acton," he added, wringing his hand. "Devilish business, this."

"I came the moment I received your message. I should appreciate it if you would fill me in."

"You know of events up to now?" At Acton's nod, he continued. "Edward and I proceeded to the address, a noisome area of town, I must say. The coach had no more than drawn to a halt than we were surrounded. I hope never to see a viler set of ruffians, but Edward's disguise served us well. It enabled us to even the odds."

"And Will?"

"Sold to a chimney sweep. We were able to beat that much out of them, but I'm afraid that was all they knew."

"It is a start, however," Acton said. "I won't hesitate to say I'm sure you have some idea of the person responsible. My man Jenks is well acquainted with my cousin's stables. It does seem likely to me he will know best whose tongue to loosen with drink. We will no doubt have news in a day or two."

"I daresay you will. If there is nothing further we can do, Acton, we'll be off."

"How can I thank you—" Jessica began.

"Don't try, ma'am. We were happy to have been of service." Lord Benchley bowed, and in another minute the gentlemen had left the room. Acton accompanied them to their coach, talked for a moment with them, and returned to the salon.

Jessica got up quickly, and ran to him. "Do you think—"

"I do," he said, taking her hand. "The case is not so very desperate, my dear."

"McClean is the most odious toad I have ever known."

"I agree that he is," said Acton, raising her fingers to his lips. "Shall we put him from our minds, Jessica? I would much rather think of you. Did you miss me?"

Jessica raised her eyes to his. "You know I did," she said softly. "Acton—?"

He stood staring down at her, a muscle jerking in his cheek. For a moment they were very still. Thoughts of casting aside every consideration of honour flickered for a moment through his mind, until, with an effort, he recalled himself. "Tell me of the entertainments you attended in my absence," he said, releasing her hand. "Did you enjoy the Leversham's ball?"

Jessica flushed. "At first I did," she managed to say. "But then—no, we aren't to speak of McClean."

His eyes narrowed. "Please do," he murmured after a pause.

She shrugged and looked away. "He suggested a divorce. Perhaps he was right."

No wrathful explosion greeted this remark. Quite to the contrary. Acton threw back his head and laughed. "Did he indeed?" he said. "He must be desperate to be so foolish."

She looked at him, frowning. "Is he?" she said quietly. "You should wonder about that."

Surprise flickered for an instant in his eyes. "I know, my dear," he said gently. "It isn't easy for me, believe me. If I could act differently, I would."

"Perhaps you will be so good as to tell me what happens now."

"Nothing, Jessica, until my name is cleared. I thought I had made that plain."

"I feel so—unloved."

His hands went out to her, then dropped to his sides. "My dear, there is nothing I want more than to take you in my arms, and prove my love. You cannot know the effort it has cost me not to touch you. The nights I have spent in hell—"

"And what of me? Cannot you know what I have endured, knowing you didn't w-want me," she said, her lip trembling. "Do you not know how a woman feels to think she isn't l-loved—"

"Dearest," he said, gathering her hands in his. "I feel sure it won't be for much longer. McClean is becoming careless, as in this affair with Will. If he was involved in the murders, and I can't help but think he might have been, he will soon make the fatal blunder."

She stared at him, round-eyed. "I never knew you thought that," she said, astonished.

Acton sighed. "You see, my dear, the evidence, though circumstantial, points to him."

"Really," she said, interested. "Why?"

He kissed her fingers. "I think it best to drop the subject. I do not mean to alarm you, Jessica, but I will request that you avoid his company."

She glanced at him, and saw he was looking gravely down at her. "I think I am beginning to understand," she murmured thoughtfully. "It isn't only your own honour, is it? McClean is family."

He again raised her fingers to his lips. "You are my family," he said softly.

"Shall you want—babies—one day?"

"One day, when we are free of our troubles. But not too soon," he hastened to add, chuckling. "I shouldn't fancy my heir in my way. Not for a time, at least."

CHAPTER IX

Three days later the butler at McClean's lodgings in Pall Mall opened the door to find a groom upon the step. "His Grace, the Duke of Acton, to call upon Lord McClean Alastair," the man pronounced in formal tones.

The butler's gaze swung to the cavalcade drawn up before the door. In front of and behind the crested coach, postilions astride magnificent horseflesh held their mounts motionless, with eyes staring straight ahead. A groom, having lowered the steps of the coach, stood back, and his Grace stepped down. A formal call, thought the butler, his eyes sweeping the liveried retainers. He bowed, and held the door wide.

Mounting the staircase, he preceded Acton down the hall. "His Grace, the Duke of Acton," he announced from the doorway of McClean's rooms.

McClean was sitting at a table before a window, scribbling on a sheet of paper. "I'm not at home," he growled without looking up.

"Ah, but I believe you are," said Acton, walking into the room. "How could you think otherwise, McClean?"

McClean turned his head. "I haven't time to see you," he muttered ungraciously. "Can't you see I'm busy?"

"I'm sure I shan't keep you," Acton replied, unruffled. "I plan to be brief. And to the point, I might add. Do you doubt it?"

Something in his voice sent a chill down McClean's spine. "Well, what is it?" he asked, casting a quick look at Acton, wondering what he had gotten wind of.

Acton appeared surprised. "But your latest ploy, dear boy. What else?"

"If you have come to speak in riddles—"

"I must be a sore trial," Acton remarked sympathetically. "I wonder you haven't attempted to do me in. Or have you?" he added quietly.

McClean picked up his pen with trembling fingers. How much does he know, damn him, he asked himself. Aloud, he said, "Your remarks distress me. Pray, what have I done to deserve them?"

"I am not quite sure as yet, McClean. But I will be. Depend upon it. I will be."

"Really, Acton, your tone—"

"Is nothing to what it will be, should I find you in town this time next week."

"Don't be absurd. Why should I leave town? The season isn't over."

"For you it is. Shall I list the reasons why? I believe not. I feel confident you will know them." Crossing to the door, Acton paused on the threshold. "I beg you to believe me when I say you will receive worse treatment at my hands than little Will received at yours, should you fail to take my meaning." With these words hanging heavily in the air, he turned on his heel and went calmly down the stairs.

He next called at Grosvenor Square. Finding Lord Benchley not at home, he dismissed his coach, and strolled on down the street and around the corner and continued on to White's. Entering the club, he looked around, and, locating Benchley, walked in his leisurely way to join him. "I stand greatly in your debt," he said sitting down.

"Oh, hardly that," Benchley grinned, taking the hand held out to him. "I enjoyed the run-in, you know. I can't think when I'd last been in a mill."

"Did not the thought of what the outcome could have been bother you?"

"Not in the least," Benchley said cheerfully. "I have a constitutional dislike of anyone who would upset the ladies, bless them. What have you heard of her Grace's tiger?"

"He is restored to us, you will be glad to know. It wasn't difficult, as I perceived. My servant plied McClean's with sufficient spirits—the man proved a veritable fount of knowledge, as a matter of fact. I merely went around to the sweep, and bought Will back."

"Had he been abused?"

"He had," Acton replied, his lips tightening. "But I didn't come here to talk of that. I won't embarrass you by prosing on about my gratitude, but you have it."

"My dear boy, you would have done the same for me," he said. "Join me for luncheon, Acton, won't you?"

Some time later, Acton excused himself and returned home. Her Grace, the butler informed him, was in her dressing room tending to young Will. The compartment, of course, opened off Jessica's room. As was customary, it contained a cot for the occasional use of her Grace's lady's maid in addition to a chair and table. At the moment it supported the diminutive form of the tiger. He had been bathed, the welts on his body doctored, and now lay gazing up at Jessica with adoration shining in his eyes. "You promise not to leave me?" he begged. "I'd be scared, if you do."

"My room is just next door, Will. You need only call, and I will hear you."

"Promise?"

"I promise. You must go to sleep now. Nothing can harm you here, so you need have no fear it will."

Acton stood watching, and then followed Jessica to her room. Closing the door firmly behind them, he turned to look at her, his gaze softened. "Shall I ever forget your tenderness?" he said, crossing to stand before her. "The way you gathered that sooty little body into your arms, with no regard for the dirt rubbing off on you. Not many ladies of your station would have done so."

"There is nothing in that," she said. "It was only my gown that was dirtied."

"No," he replied, pulling her into his arms. 'It was concern for the suffering of a fellow human being. I have never adored you more than I do at this moment."

Jessica flushed happily. "Her Grace thanks his Grace for the compliment," she murmured softly.

For a moment he held her close, looking down into her eyes, and then his lips claimed hers. Jessica melted against him, and rubbed her body sensuously against his. Acton's head jerked up. "To hell with it!" he muttered to himself, and bent to her again.

His lips grew passionate, demanding, as he kissed

her again and again. Groaning deep within his throat, he swept her off her feet, and carried her to the bed. "Jessica, Jessica," he murmured huskily, his fingers busy with the buttons of her bodice. A little voice speaking from the doorway drew his head around. "Damn!" he swore. The tiger was standing there.

"Ma'am?" piped Will. "I'm scared."

"He is just a baby, Acton," Jessica whispered, slipping from the bed. "He's been through a frightening experience."

"So are we to have no privacy? I'll put a lock on that door. See if I don't."

"Shh," she cautioned, crossing to take Will by the hand. "You mustn't be afraid," she told him, leading him away.

Some fifteen minutes passed before she was free to return to her room. She paused on the threshold, the tears coming into her eyes. Acton had gone. Crossing slowly to the bed, she sank down on it. It was not surprising, she thought drearily. She might as well have doused him with cold water. But he *had* succumbed, she mused, her spirits rising. If he would do so once, he would do so again.

CHAPTER X

Acton slowly descended the stairs, a black domino over his arm, a mask dangling from his fingers. The fact that the time was close on eleven bothered him not in the least. Knowing his Jessica very well, he proceeded on his leisurely way across the hall, to surrender the domino and mask into a footman's keeping. "Inform her Grace I await her in the library," he said, and went into the room. He was well aware that public ridottos were frowned upon by older members of the ton, and knew he himself might not care for it. But Jessica had argued so prettily for the idea that he had reluctantly agreed. He should, without exerting himself unduly, be able to steer her clear of any ungenteel excesses occurring during the affair.

At this moment, the door opened, and Jessica came dancing in. "Here you are, Acton," she cooed, whirling about with a silk domino held up under her chin. "Isn't it thrilling? I shall dance, and flirt, and no one will be the wiser."

"So you will flirt, will you?" Acton said, taking the

domino from her hands. "May I inquire the identity of this so fortunate man?"

"How churlish of you," she said, going off on a peal of entrancing laughter. "Well, sir, I shan't tell you."

"If you have quite finished, my dear, shall we be on our way?" he replied tranquilly. "I trust you plan to arrive before midnight."

Jessica was enchanted with the ridotto from the moment she set eyes on it. Couples in gaily coloured dominos moved to the strains of music in a pavilion built for dancing, while other laughing celebrants strolled along well-lit garden paths. "Do let's dance," she begged," tugging at his hand. "Only see how much fun it is, Acton. I'm so glad we came."

His eyes smiled at her through the slits in his mask. "Do I say yes to the dancing, or to the fun?" he asked teasingly.

"Silly," she said, and turned to lead the way. The dance floor was by now thronged with people, but Jessica could discern nothing in anyone's demeanour to raise eyebrows. We might as well be at Almack's, she thought, and giggled. That nothing occurred to shock her was entirely due to Acton. He accompanied her only to those areas of the gardens free from roistering, and made certain she remained unaware of what was taking place in curtained alcoves opening off the ballroom.

They partook of ham slivers and champagne in one of the boxes at two o'clock in the morning. Jessica's eyes glowed behind her mask as she teased Acton, and merrily joined him in toasting everything that came into their heads. Returning to the ballroom they danced the hours away, oblivious to the world around them. When finally they took their departure, Jessica looked back and sighed. "It was such a perfect evening," she murmured softly. "I hate for it to end."

"I, too, sweetheart," he agreed, a gentle smile hovering about his mouth. "You may be sure we will repeat it."

She expected their carriage to convey them immediately home, but to her surprise Acton instructed McCauley to drive them through Hyde Park. In the quiet of early morning, it seemed to her that an enchantment hung over the sleeping city. Held cozily against his side, she felt his lips against her hair, and snuggled closer still. His fingers beneath her chin lifted her face to the growing glow of morn. "Who is to see?" he murmured against her lips, and continued kissing her until they drew up before the house.

Jessica awoke at noon, some nagging little thought tugging at the fringes of her mind. Then she remembered, and shivered in delight. Of course, she thought. Her plan. The carriage had put the idea into her head, during that enchanted interlude with Acton in the early hours of the dawn.

Sitting up in bed, she gazed dreamily into space, pondering her problem. Were she to flee in one vehicle, would Acton follow in another? Jessica felt much inclined to think he would. Only the details needed resolving for the plan to be put into action. She was determined to break her husband's barrier of restraint.

If Acton was aware of her preoccupation during the coming days, he failed to mention it. He was often in her company and, though his eyes rested broodingly on her face at times, he made no move to touch her. The arrival of a parcel came at a time when Jessica, in low spirits, and so naturally finding it impossible to resist, had purchased the most ravishing, and costly, confection of a bonnet, only to find that she already had quite decided she thoroughly detested it. Feeling the most miserable spendthrift alive, and expecting Acton's disapproval, she was now prepared to pronounce the very laudable intention of mending her ways.

When Acton dropped the package in her lap, therefore, she was much at a loss. She hadn't precisely determined how she could possibly explain Madame Francel's latest bill, much less understand how she could accept anything further from him with anything vaguely approaching a clear conscience. "Open it," he said, and stood waiting expectantly.

Jessica stared, dismayed, at the collection of jewels nestling in the box. Emeralds glittered and winked in the light, leering at her most evilly. More embarrassed than she could ever remember having been, she said, weakly, "They are lovely, Acton."

"Are you not pleased, my dear?" he asked, the hurt in his tone. "You don't sound particularly enthusiastic."

"Acton, I had better tell you at once I've done something that will make you very angry. You won't want to give me jewels when you know," she concluded tragically.

"Then I must reserve my tantrum until I do," he said gravely, but with a smile quivering about his lips.

"I assure you it isn't amusing," she said in one of her rare bursts of candor. "I don't know why I did it. It isn't as though it were a pretty bonnet, Acton. In fact, it is the horridest thing imaginable."

"I fail to perceive your problem, my dear. Throw it away."

"But—the bill—" She took a deep breath. "—the price was enormous," she finished in a rush.

"I trust you do not intend instructing me in how

I should spend my money, Jessica. If your allowance has proven insufficient for your needs, I will increase it."

"Increase it!" she squeaked. "It's too much already."

He laughed, and lifted the necklace from the box. "Bend your head," he said, placing it about her neck and fastening the clasp. It was naturally impossible for him to touch her without lightly trailing his fingers around the stones, and by so doing sending shivers down her spine as he stroked the flesh around her bosom. Jerking his fingers back as if they were scorched, he said, "Wear them to Almack's tonight, with, I believe, your gold gown," and quickly left the room.

She was not without hope for her current plan, and had every intention of seeking the company of Mr. Wardly, should he be in attendance at Almack's. When late into the entertainment she perceived him enter, she cast him a smile that brought him to her side. Accepting with an eagerness all out of proportion to his request, she curtsied and told him she would most surely enjoy the pleasure of a dance with him. Glancing slyly at Acton, and seeing the expression on his face, she smiled to herself and went off on Mr. Wardly's arm to take her place in the set that was forming. Never one to await an opportunity, much preferring instead to create one of her own, she immediately said in a conversational way, "I have noticed you seldom use your coach around London, Mr. Wardly. Do you dislike it?"

"Dislike it?" he repeated puzzled. "I can't say that I do. Why do you ask?"

"My deplorable curiosity, sir. It has ever been a fault with me."

"On the contrary," he replied. "Will it gratify you to know that you have no faults?"

"You must allow me to refute that statement," she smiled. "I was glad to see you here tonight, Mr. Wardly. You have stood my friend before. Is it too terribly forward of me to hope you will do so again?"

"What a ridiculous question, Lady Jessica. How may I serve you?"

"You may lend me your coach, if it would not inconvenience you. I find I must journey into Sussex to visit at the bedside of an ailing relative. It seems Acton will require our coach, and I find myself in need of transportation."

"I shall be gratified to place my coach at your disposal. When do you plan to leave?"

"I should be on my way by ten o'clock tomorrow morning. I do appreciate your generosity, Mr. Wardly, and assure you your coach will be returned by nightfall."

"I could not consider letting you journey forth alone," he said, smiling. "I am honoured to offer you my protection."

Jessica gave a start. "That will not be necessary," she said positively. "My maid and my tiger will accompany me. I do thank you, however, for your kind offer."

"One lone female and one small boy for company cannot signify. You will be glad of a man along, should the need arise for one."

Jessica was thinking fast. She had singled out Mr. Wardly, knowing full well a gentleman of more years and experience would not consider for one minute such a subterfuge. Short of revealing her plans, nothing would stop him from tagging along. Acton would be furious. Well, so much the better. He could then be depended upon to set out in hot pursuit. She need only contrive to be free of Mr. Wardly before Acton caught up with her. "Perhaps you are right," she said, seeming to ponder. "Are you certain the hour of departure will not inconvenience you in any way?"

"Quite certain. I often rise at an early hour."

"There is one thing more," Jessica murmured, glancing at him. "I will ask you to keep the journey secret."

"Secret!" he uttered, staring hard at her.

"You see," she began, desperately searching her mind. "Acton has an appointment tomorrow which is most important. Should he know of this, he would feel obliged to cancel it to accompany me. That would be foolish, as I'm sure you realize. I will return home by late afternoon, in any event."

He considered this. "Are you quite certain his Grace will approve of your going off without him? For if he won't—"

"If I thought he would disapprove, I should not think of considering it," she insisted somewhat breathlessly.

"Well, in that case," he said, reassured, "I will be before your door at the appointed hour."

Jessica wisely spoke next of something quite different, chattering on until the dance came to an end, and she could return on his arm to rejoin Acton. Seizing the opportunity, she murmured, while watching Mr. Wardly move away, "He is handsome, wouldn't you say, Acton?"

"It was obvious you thought so from the way you smiled at him," he replied without any noticeable degree of censure in his tone.

Nettled, she continued, "Just see how his coat sits his shoulders. He must be an athlete, for them to be so broad."

He glanced quizzically down at her. "Do you think so?" he asked, maddeningly calm.

"I'm persuaded it accounts for his success in turning the ladies up sweet. He has sufficient address, of course, but a handsome appearance must always be regarded as an asset."

"I know I shouldn't say it, my dear, but I do have your measure, you know. You need not continue prosing about young Wardly."

"You might speak in less obscure terms, Acton," she said with spirit. "How am I to know what you mean?"

"I think you do. In any event, I shan't pander to you by explaining it."

She shot an indignant look at him. "You have acquired a most irritating habit of putting me in the wrong. And that, I might add, does not please me in the least."

He smiled. "I beg your pardon for fanning the flame. But you see, my dear, I found myself quite unable to resist the temptation. It was an overpowering one, believe me."

"Are you laughing at me?" she shot at him. "For if you are, I think it shocking."

"You must forgive me, Jessica. I realize Wardly is a prime favorite with you—as well he should be. I am not insensible to his role in rescuing Will, but you will allow we have little in common."

"I do, but why must you tease me?" she asked, not in the least mollified.

"Merely for the pleasure of seeing you fire up, my dear, and to demonstrate that you cannot gull me."

She lowered her eyes, and attempted to maintain a stern countenance. Failing, she laughed softly. "My experience with you, sir, has led me to believe you are abominable."

"While my experience with you, my dear, has led me to know your tongue is a weapon. Albeit an adorable one."

It was fortunate for Jessica that Lord Lester came up at that moment to request the pleasure of a dance, for she was quite unable to think of a suitable reply. Left alone, Acton stood gazing after her with an expression of longing in his eyes that was hard to read.

"Why so glum?" Lord Ames said cheerfully, coming up and clapping him on the back. "You must be indulging in depressing thoughts."

Acton's attention had been so fixed on Jessica that he had not noticed his friend's approach, but he now turned his head and said somewhat cryptically, "If you knew my thoughts at this moment, Jules, you would think me demented."

CHAPTER XI

How to dispense with Mr. Wardly's presence at the appropriate moment occupied Jessica's mind for no little time after she first retired to bed for those few hours still remaining of the night. Discarding several alternative plans as being too involved to hold any expectation of success, she was forced to conclude that a simple solution was what she sought. It was really too provoking. Had Mr. Wardly simply offered to send his coach around, she need only order his coachman to put about at any time it suited her to do so. She could not, however, fault Mr. Wardly. She might resent his interference in her schemes, but she was using him abominably, and she knew it. The only salve she could find for her conscience lay in her determination to keep him in ignorance of having served Acton an undeserved turn. She would (in the words employed by Will) "spin a yarn." Her cousin would be made to reside some few miles out from Wigglesford. The property being located amid so tangled a maze of roadways as to make finding it a virtual impossibility, arrangement had gone forward for her to put up at the local inn, with the fictitious cousin providing transport for the remainder of the way. Mr. Wardly's services, therefore, upon their arrival at the inn, would no longer be required. Jessica added one final touch. Acton, his business transacted, would duly arrive to escort her home.

Agnes, as might have been expected, displayed marked signs of wanting to serve notice when informed of her own role in the adventure. She said, among other things, while begging her Grace's pardon, that she had long deprecated hoydenish conduct, and for a topper, that she would be hard put to explain such intolerable behaviour to his Grace. Whereupon Jessica blithely brushed aside such cowardly considerations, assuring Agnes she would hardly be called upon to explain anything, and, in the way of a topper of her own, that any recriminations that fell would surely fall upon her own head. Will, of course, was entranced with the whole idea.

Jessica had exercised care in setting the hour of departure. Conversant with Acton's morning schedule, she knew his phaeton was ordered for nine o'clock. She further knew, by the simple expedient of questioning his secretary, that he intended not returning until sometime after three. Not wanting to leave anything to chance, she stood by her front window at nine to witness his departure. A tiny smile curling her lips, she then instructed Agnes in the packing of a valise, sent the maid to pack her own and Will's, with instructions to appear downstairs some few minutes before ten.

And so when Mr. Wardly drew up before the door, Jessica immediately descended the steps and entered the coach. She paid no heed to the disapproval in

Saunders' eyes—indeed in his whole bearing—but occupied herself for the next moments in seeing Agnes and Will settled into the seat facing Mr. Wardly and herself. The groom let up the steps, climbed to his seat, and in another instant they were away.

The highway to Cromsley ran along the base of low hills on its way to Henders, before turning sharply left, and thus on to Wigglesford. They encountered little traffic, as Jessica noted with satisfaction. Beyond a curricle and a farmer's cart on its way to market, which they passed with ease, an accommodation coach coming in the opposite direction was the only conveyance seen. Its appearance made ludicrous by baggage piled atop its roof, the cumbersome vehicle swayed and lurched from side to side in the center of the road, forcing Mr. Wardly's coachman to come abreast of it with his wheels periously close to the edge. Safely by it, they proceeded on another mile to the Abbington turnpike. The groom had the yard of tin conveniently to hand, and blew up for the pike, much to Will's delight. Jessica made no effort to restrain him. A likelier means for leaving a trail than a black boy hanging from the window would be difficult to imagine. Acton would encounter no difficulty at all in discovering their route of progress.

Inside the coach Agnes sat stiff as a ramrod. If her Grace did not know what was due her consequence, there were those who did. To think that her own presence could lend countenance to the escapade— well, she knew what his Grace would have to say. As for his lordship seated across from her, she recognized a rascal when she saw one. The gentleman in question seemed not to notice he was being stigmatized. To label him a rascal seemed unjust, for, although he

was certainly dressed in the height of fashion, there
was nothing of the dandy in his demeanour. Quite the
reverse. He sat beside Jessica, talking pleasantly on
any number of subjects, and in general made himself
agreeable.

Jessica, when the coach drew up before the inn,
allowed Mr. Wardly to hand her down and, by the
simple expedient of holding out her hand, put a
period to his insistence on remaining by her side. The
inn proved to be quite ancient and, as was customary
with structures of its date, half-timbered. Jessica engaged two chambers, one for Agnes and Will, and
one for herself, and sent them to the floor above with
instructions to unpack her valise. She had no difficulty
in procuring the private parlour, bespoke tea, and
went upstairs to remove the stains of travel from her
face.

The afternoon dragged past without bringing Acton.
Jessica went out front several times, only to experience
disappointment. The inn, situated as it was at the
top of the hill, afforded an excellent view of the village and of the road beyond. But so far as she could
discover, no vehicle made use of it, neither Acton's
nor anyone else's. It was shortly before dinnertime
when his phaeton pulled into the coachyard. Almost
immediately his step was heard approaching the parlour. "Here you are, my dear," he said, coming into
the room. "Did you have a pleasant journey?"

Jessica glanced at him, assessing his mood. Unless
she was very much mistaken, he appeared amused. "I
didn't enjoy it all that much," she admitted ingenu-
ously.

"Perhaps—forgive me, Jessica, if I mistake your
meaning—would you rather have been with me?"

Jessica flushed. There could be no doubt. He was amused. "I'm afraid my words misled you. Your appearance surprised me, just for a moment."

"Could you see your way clear to improve upon that statement, my dear? I believe that I am still quite at sea."

"You are laughing at me," she told him accusingly. "I am sorry to have to say it, but you are being rude."

"My deplorable upbringing," he agreed, taking a chair facing hers. "You will forgive the question, my dear, but why did you feel you must put me to the trouble of following you? Had I displeased you in some way?"

Jessica assumed an air of innocence. "I, sir?" she said on a note of inquiry. "It did not occur to me you would set out in pursuit."

"That would account, no doubt, for the care with which you marked your passing."

Jessica gasped. "You are very wrong if you think that, Acton. I came to visit a cousin who is ill."

At that a chuckle escaped him. "You have no cousin," he reminded her relentlessly. "I hesitate to press you, my dear, but I am waiting for an answer."

Jessica looked away. "I am afraid you have been put to a great deal of trouble," she murmured, thinking hard. "Actually, I am enroute to lend my support to a friend. Her mother has been taken gravely ill, and—and Lizzie sent for me." Her eyes returned to his face, "You do believe me, Acton, do you not?" she asked expectantly.

"I would not phrase it quite like that," he said. "You do seem to have acquired a surfeit of ill acquaintances, would you not say? I can only admire your—humane impulses in responding so speedily."

Jessica, trapped, ventured to say, "I have never spoken of it before, but from a child I was taught that to sacrifice oneself for one's friends is the noblest of virtues."

"Honesty was no doubt among the virtues you were taught? But of course it would have been."

She could no longer meet his eyes. Her own wandered to her slippers peeping out from under her gown; she gazed at them as if seeing them for the first time. "I'm afraid I did set out to hoax you," she admitted, her voice low. "You understood that from the beginning, didn't you?"

"Certainly," he said, preserving his calm.

She raised eyes full of resolution to his. "It was not a very sensible thing to do," she said, flustered.

"Not very," he agreed, with only the suspicion of a smile twitching at the corners of his lips.

Jessica's curiosity got the better of her. "When did you know?" she had to ask.

"The moment Saunders told me. I have only one quarrel to pick with you, Jessica. Must it have been young Wardly?"

"I thought he might have made you jealous," she said frankly.

"Not in the least," replied Acton. "Surely you could have found someone other than a beardless youth? My vanity is bruised."

Jessica saw the gleam in his eyes, and laughed in spite of herself. "I felt uneasy about it at the time. I will need to do better, in future."

"In future, my dear, you will concentrate on me." So saying, he rose and crossed to the door. "You may be interested to know your wardrobe has been dispatched to Aynesworth. Also Lottie. I thought it best to leave your curricle in town. The countryside is not yet prepared for the sight of Will in his outlandish garb."

Jessica felt a sudden constriction in her chest. Her lips quivered. "Where a-are you g-going?"

"To engage a chamber," he said, brows raised.

She felt dizzy with relief. "But Acton—I mean—your business—"

"The devil with my business," he said, and went out.

Twenty minutes later he returned to the parlour, to find Jessica waiting beside the fire. "I trust you are hungry, Acton," she said, smiling up at him. "You will let me know if the meal I have ordered pleases you?"

"I will let you know in due time what pleases me," he said somewhat enigmatically. "Shall we be seated?"

She crossed to the table, and took the chair at his right which he pulled back for her. "The soups looks good," she remarked unfolding her napkin.

Acton regarded her steadily. "Do not tell me that, in the rush of your day's activities, you forgot to eat."

"No, indeed," she said, picking up her spoon. "I had a quite substantial tea."

"Which consisted of—?" he asked, looking at her over the rim of his wine glass.

A startled look came into her eyes; the effort to remember brought a crease between her brows. "Do you know, Acton, you are very astute," she said, finally. "I do believe I forgot all about it."

He set his glass down, and frowned. "Your conclusions are ill-founded, my dear. I need not be astute to see you are careless where your own welfare is concerned."

"It is worse than I thought," she remarked, drinking her soup. "You intend being the mother hen, with me your chick."

"The role may be new to me, Jessica, but I trust I can play it. My repertoire is most adaptable."

"As is mine. You are not eating, Acton."

"It is more than likely," he told her softly, "that you will shortly discover just how adaptable my roles can be."

She threw him a saucy look. "Then I would be wise to recruit my strength," she said pertly.

"I shouldn't advise you to dally overly long in doing so," he remarked urbanely, slicing her a piece of ham. "You could go to bed hungry."

Much to Jessica's surprise, she blushed. "You draw an enticing portrait, your Grace, but I can assure you that, whatever your intentions may be, mine are to finish my dinner."

"Pray do," he replied, placing roast potato upon her plate. "Shall you care for peas?"

A laugh escaped Jessica. "I shall," she said, and began to eat with relish. Acton did not say very much during the remainder of the dinner, though he responded readily enough to her remarks. When finally the meal drew to its conclusion, and he ceased speaking at all, but sat watching her, she felt compelled to say, "You are so quiet, Acton. What are you thinking about?"

"You. Without your clothes."

"Acton!"

"You asked me."

She looked away, and knew that his gaze never wavered from her face. When he spoke, she started. "Since the covers were removed, you have eaten a

peach, some assorted nuts, and a pear. Are you attempting to draw out the meal?"

A smile trembled on her lips. "The landlord went
to so much trouble, I thought I should do it justice,"
she said. "I have never known anyone so bent on getting his own way, my lord. You'd be well served if
I denied you my bed."

"While you, my own, would receive your just deserts
if I took you at your word."

Turning her head so that she could look him full in
the face, she smiled at him with so much tenderness
that she took his breath away. "There is not the
smallest need for you to fear I will," she said truthfully. "You would pay me no heed, in any event."

"None whatever," he admitted. "I should myself
not choose to pursue you like some young cawker
barely out of leading strings, but if you prefer it, I
suppose I could."

"I rather fancy I shouldn't care for that any more
than you. Acton," she said after a moment. "Weren't
you a little jealous of Mr. Wardly?"

"Damnably so."

Jessica laughed happily. "For one who claims to be
omniscient, your Grace," she said in a teasing voice,
"you can be sadly ill-informed."

"Can I now?" he replied softly. "Surely you do not
flatter yourself to the extent of believing that every
man who crosses your path finds he must lay his heart
at your feet?"

"I made sure you thought so."

"I could call your bluff, my dear. Being a gentleman, however, I will only inform you it was not Mr.
Wardly's person I took objection to. It was his being
in your confidence that loosed the beast in me."

She glanced at him, startled. "I did not take him

into my confidence," she said, eyes round. "I made sure he thought I was enroute to visit a relative."

Acton studied her. "Perhaps you had better let me know just what you did tell him," he said pensively.

"It isn't all that bad," she assured him, gazing at him hopefully. "I told him you required the use of our coach, and asked to borrow his. I'm sorry, Acton, but he would tag along."

"For the purpose of offering his protection," he said in his dryest tones.

"Well, yes. But I told him you would insist upon accompanying me, should you learn of it."

His smile was twisted. "Thank you, my dear," he said. "I should hate to think I would fail to extend my own protection."

"Well, at least I told him you were to meet me here, for the purpose of escorting me home."

"It is quite unnecessary to tell me that, my dear. Of course I would be made to put in an appearance, albeit a tardy one. What an enlivening time you must have had."

A silence fell. Conscious of the irony in his tone, she averted her face. "I own it must sound as if I had, but it so happens I regretted it almost from the start."

"I'm glad to hear you admit it," he drawled calmly. "Now we can be comfortable again."

"Well!" she said wrathfully, turning the full force of her gaze on him. "Here I am trying to explain— yes, and to apologize—and all you can find to do is talk in a perfectly odious fashion!"

"Come, come, my dear. It is unladylike to quarrel. Where is your sense of decorum?" His eyes alive with mischief, he added, "That wasn't quite fair of me, was it? For just a moment there, I forgot you had put yourself to a deal of trouble in bringing me here."

"Now, that is going too far," she said, lips held firmly prim. "I am persuaded you didn't forget it for a moment."

"How right you are," he remarked, and grinned. "You may have noticed it is pouring rain? Our departure in the morning may be delayed."

"Oh," said Jessica, digesting this. "Well, I shan't mind. I have rather a strong liking for this place."

What he would have replied to this was forever lost in the commotion occasioned by a party of people crowding into the inn. The accommodation coach, it seemed, had become mired down, forcing its passengers to seek shelter from the storm. Acton, swearing softly under his breath, turned his head in surprise as a stout woman of indeterminate age helped herself to a seat at his table. "There's no need to worry ourselves," she told him cheerfully. "All in God's good time, is what I say."

"Good Lord!" Acton ejaculated, stunned at her impudence.

"Amen to that," she nodded, motioning to someone out of Acton's vision. "Over here, Mr. Tomms," she called above the babel of voices. "Set yourself right down here beside me."

An admonitory kick against his ankle brought Acton's eyes to Jessica's face. "We seem to have acquired guests," she murmured softly, eyes brimful with laughter. "Do not raise a fuss, I beg you."

"Then you do not mind?" he asked her quietly.

"Not a bit," she replied, looking up as a man who appeared to be a travelling salesman took the chair next to the stout woman.

"Man and boy I have never seen the like," Mr. Tomms volunteered, shaking his head in disbelief. "I told Mrs. Simpson here it would rain, but I expected nothing like this. We're stuck here until it slacks."

"Ah, well," Mrs. Simpson said, patting his hand. "The company can't be held to blame, and we ought to get a good meal out of it."

Jessica looked interested, as indeed she was. "You are passengers from the accommodation coach?" she asked, her smile inviting confidences.

"We are," Mrs. Simpson answered, adding that it was a caution the way the company crowded so many passengers inside. In her opinion, she said, the trouble lay in selling tickets to just anyone who could pay the fare. "Now take him," she added, pointing to a fellow traveler striving to go unnoticed on the fringe of the crowd. "He's one as would rob his own Mum."

Acton, running an eye over the man, wholeheartedly agreed. He had a shifty look to him, with crafty eyes, and a way of not drawing attention to himself. Acton thought it probable he was well known to the Bow Street Runners. "I trust," he remarked, "we will not be forced to endure his company."

In this he was mistaken. The landlord, full of apologies and stammering entreaty, scurried around the room, explaining his lack of bedchambers, and begging the party to double up. Coming to a halt before Acton, he said, "If your honour has no objection, the men could share your honour's chamber, seeing as there are two beds in it. Then if your wife, maybe, could take her servants in with her, the other women could take their room."

Refusal trembled for a moment on Acton's tongue before, resigning himself to the inevitable, he nodded his head, and rose to pull back Jessica's chair. Escorting her to the foot of the stairs, he kindled the bedroom candle at one guttering on the newel post, and handed it to her. "I wish I knew what your thoughts are," she remarked, looking mischievously at him.

"I know you do," he said grimly, and stepped back. "Go on up to bed, Jessica, before I tell you."

"I promise you they wouldn't shock me."

"They would me," he told her frankly, and, turning on his heel, went back into the parlour.

CHAPTER XII

Roosters crowing in the distance awakened Jessica. The rain had ceased, and though the air was still misty the sun was just beginning to break through the clouds. She slid cautiously out of bed without disturbing Agnes, who hugged the edge even in sleep, nor Will on his cot in the corner, and quickly dressed. Twitching her skirts into place, she tiptoed to the door and went from the room. On her arrival downstairs, she found the landlord in a foul mood. Never in his fifteen years as innkeeper, he gave her to understand, had anything to equal the present invasion come in his way. One shouldn't be expected to endure half so much. As to when breakfast would be served, he couldn't say. In the meantime, she might wish to stroll about outside.

Jessica went without demur. The sun was by now shining brightly, with not a cloud to be seen in the sky. She wandered around the side of the inn, and past the stables, to a path leading off across a field. Following it to a wood, she found the air cooler under the trees and sat down for a time, listening dreamily to a bird singing somewhere overhead. A rabbit scuttling across the path behind her brought her head around. She had thought herself alone, and so was not prepared to see the villainous-looking passenger from the accommodation coach standing there staring at her intently, an inquiring look in his eyes. Chilled to the marrow, she caught her breath on a cry and fled back along the path to the inn. She rushed inside and sank onto a chair in the parlour fighting for breath.

At this moment the door opened and Acton walked in. His brows shot up. "Perhaps you will be so good as to tell me why the covers have not been laid," he said to the landlord just entering from the common room.

"If your honour permits, we are all at sixes in the kitchens this morning," the landlord whined.

Acton put up his quizzing glass, and surveyed him through it. "I do not in the least understand," he remarked, "what that has to do with your failure to procure our breakfast. See to it."

"Will y'honour favour an omelet, and perhaps a bit of bacon?"

"I should not think I could be expected to formulate your menu," Acton replied, and went across to the table. Pulling out a chair next to the one in which Jessica was seated, he sat down somewhat heavily.

Jessica cast him a critical glance. "You did not pass a restful night," she remarked.

"I haven't the slightest doubt you did," he shot back, frowning. "I shall presently have something to say to you on the subject of our being in this place. For now, I would appreciate your silence."

"You have a headache," she calmly returned. "You will feel better with some breakfast."

He made an effort to choke back a retort, and failed. "I suppose," he said sardonically, "there should be some way to stop a female from chattering."

Jessica subsided. Nor did she say anything from the time the landlord at last placed their meal before them, until they finished it. Acton then pulled back her chair and assisted her to her feet. Still without speaking, he put his hand under her elbow and escorted her outside. Eyeing the phaeton waiting before the door, she said, "What of Agnes and Will?"

"I will send the carriage for them when we arrive at Aynesworth," he answered shortly. "No harm will come to them, and Agnes will perhaps learn not to assist you in annoying me in future."

"Surely you aren't putting the blame on her!" Jessica exclaimed.

"Not at all. Or rather, not all of it. I am perfectly aware who most deserves my censure."

"You are the most idiotic creature I have ever known," she cried, a break in her voice.

"I seem to have heard you say as much before, though odious is the term you usually employ. If your memory is at all retentive, my dear, you will recall the instances."

This way of laying the facts before her was scarcely calculated to mollify her, any more than acknowledging to herself that she was again at fault could soothe her temper. "I am not at all sure I shan't wait here with Agnes and Will," she said flatly.

"I am much afraid that—this once—you will do as I say," he replied, and walked forward to wait beside the phaeton. "Do not put me to the trouble of fetching you," he added, regarding her levelly.

Jessica muttered something under her breath that in a lady of lesser stature would have sounded much like an oath, and allowed him to hand her up. Glancing at her as he swung up into the phaeton and stepped across her to his seat, he set the greys forward. She very much would have liked giving him a piece of her mind but she controlled the unladylike impulse, knowing it useless, and kept her lips pressed tightly together. For perhaps two miles she remained determined in her purpose. The struggle, however, became intolerable. Her colour rose, but she ventured to say, "It is a lovely morning, is it not?"

Acton turned his head. "In God's name, Jessica, what possessed you?" he said, looking at her with a mixture of questioning and bewilderment in his eyes. "Do you not realize the scandal this escapade could give rise to? We can only hope no slanderous tongue gets wind of it."

"I shouldn't think they would," she said hopefully. "I didn't give my true identity at the inn. I thought it clever of me not to disclose it."

There came a moment's silence. The faintest of smiles appeared on his lips. "You abominable little rattle-pate," he said reprovingly. "I should shake you for the night I have just endured."

Jessica blinked at him. "Was it so very much a trial?" she asked tentatively.

"It isn't as if having gallows bait thrust upon me were not enough; Mr. Tomms needs must snore loud enough to rouse the dead."

She thought it best to say, "I'm sorry," and to add after a moment, "Do you really think the—the one man is—a criminal?"

"I should imagine him no stranger to the police."

A constriction in her throat made it impossible for her to say anything further. It was not necessary in any event, for a bend in the road brought a coach into view. Acton sent the greys thundering down upon it, increasing rather than slackening their wicked pace. "Blow up a blast," he said, nodding toward the yard of tin.

"Surely you don't intend going around it?" she gasped. "You will land us in the ditch."

"Blow it up," he repeated, grinning. "I know that coach."

Jessica, afraid of distracting him, did as he bade. Feeling weak with apprehension, she stared at the rear of the vehicle looming up fast before them, and prayed it would pull over. Instead of doing anything of the kind, it moved to the crown of the road. "So," Acton chuckled, holding his horses in readiness to pass. "We shall see."

"Good Lord!" Jessica breathed. "You must stop this, Acton. You cannot know who it is, and—"

"Ah, but I do," he said, and chuckled. "It's Grandmama."

"Grandmama! Can you mean she knows that we—"

"She does," he said. "She will be forced to the left around the next bend. Be ready."

"You cannot mean to pass her there! Acton, for heaven's sake. Do not attempt it!"

"Just hold on," he replied, his eyes studying the road ahead. They neared the bend, and the more cumbersome coach was forced to hug the left. Even at that Jessica thought the road too narrow, but Acton calmly awaited the chance to open out his leaders. She had just decided he would not chance it when he dropped his hands. Terrified, she watched as they shot around Grandmama with scant inches to spare, and thundered on. Acton glanced back over his shoulder, and raised his hat in salute. "That should hold her," he said, with no little satisfaction.

Jessica suddenly found the use of her tongue. "I thought sure we would lock wheels," she said tartly. "That is the second fright I have had this morning, and I have no intention of sustaining a further one. If you cannot drive sensibly, you may set me down."

"We were in no danger of locking wheels," he assured her absently. "What do you mean, you have sustained a second fright?"

Her heart sank, for she had not intended mentioning it. In the heat of the moment her tongue had quite run away with her. Putting a brave face on it, she said, "I took a stroll out of doors before breakfast, and that horrible man—you know the one—followed me."

He stared at her, astounded. "Why did you not tell me?" he demanded, his expression alarmingly grim.

"I wasn't all that certain his presence was not a coincidence. He was watching me, I admit, but he could have been only curious."

"There must have been something, if you were frightened."

"I expect it was his eyes."

Acton, stunned as much by her lack of care as by her failure to mention the danger, remained for some moments in frowning silence. "My God!" he said suddenly. "Why didn't I think of it before? I wondered what a man of his stripe was doing in this neighbourhood, but it didn't occur to me—Jessica, you are not to venture out alone. It is entirely too dangerous."

"But of course," she said. "I will do much better to entrust my safety to you. You, after all, do not drive me about in a hell-for-leather fashion."

"Don't be a ninny," he advised her. "You have never been in the least danger while I held the ribbons. I won't reopen the subject of what could have happened when you were holding them yourself—enough has been said on that head."

"Indeed, it has. You know very well I was never more shaken in my life. I would never again take out your phaeton, even if I had the chance."

"You won't have the chance, my girl. A pretty figure I should cut, forever chasing after runaway teams. And another thing. I don't know where you learned such an expression as hell-for-leather, nor do I think I choose to know, but you will refrain from using it in future."

Her eyes sparkled gleefully. "Can't you think of anything other than my misadventures?" she said with a smug little smile. "What of your own, sir? Don't think I don't know you once escorted an actress to a ball, and passed her off as a lady?"

"Good Lord!" he ejaculated, startled. "How did you hear of that?"

"Grandmama told me."

"Did she also tell you I was only twenty at the time?"

"That cannot signify. It only goes to show I have but followed in your footsteps."

"Very clever," he said. "I need not remind you I am no longer a youth. I am quite grown up, thank you, and capable of controlling you."

Jessica succumbed to her emotions, bursting into laughter. "If you could but hear yourself," she gasped, searching fruitlessly in her reticule.

"Depend upon it, I will one day throttle you," he said, taking his eyes from the road ahead to glance down at her. "You will find mine in my coat pocket."

"Thank you," she said, reaching in her hand. Bringing out his handkerchief, she wiped her eyes, and held it out to him.

Eyeing the sodden square of linen with revulsion,

he raised his brows. "That, my love, I refuse to accept, even from you," he said with resolution.

This remark pleased rather than chastised her. "How you can endure all I have burdened you with in the past twenty-four hours is beyond me," she said, with unruffled composure.

"You are sunk almost beyond reproach. See you remember it."

"Come, sir. A threat? You can do better than that." Her eyes gleamed. "There's no saying what I might be tempted to do in answer to such a challenge."

"I might have known you would say something of the sort. In future, when I am unable to keep you within my sight, I will see to it that someone does. And when you object, as I know you will, I will remind you of this little chat."

"Good heavens. Are we back to that?" she exclaimed impatiently. "You must think me the worst kind of flibber-ti-gibbet."

"I do, but there's no need to raise grouse over it," he replied, feather-edging a corner. "I would be a poor sort indeed if I failed to look after you."

By this time the phaeton had reached the gates of Aynesworth. Since Jessica had become absorbed in reflections that left her feeling quite like one of those flighty females whom she much despised for forever getting themselves into situations from which they were incapable of extricating themselves, and Acton's attention was engaged in restraining the greys from bolting for the stables, both of them had fallen silent. It was not, therefore, until the phaeton drew to a halt before the house, that Jessica said "Where do you suppose Grandmama is headed?"

"Here, unless I am much mistaken," Acton replied,

jumping to the ground, and holding out his hand to assist her down. "It should be at least an hour, possibly two, before she arrives, however."

Jessica, cheered by the thought of tea before a roaring fire, thankfully mounted the front steps beside him. "Will she stay long, do you think?" she asked as they crossed the threshold.

"Not above two days, I shouldn't imagine," he replied, surrendering his beaver hat and greatcoat into the porter's keeping.

Jessica, going with him into the library, crossed to the fire, and stripped the gloves from her hands. Extending them toward the blaze, she said, "I will admit to being puzzled why she would come so far unless she intended staying a while. The journey must be quite an undertaking for a person of her years."

Acton, coming up behind her, put his hands on her shoulders, and bent to plant a kiss on her nape. "Never attempt to second-guess Grandmama, sweet. Are you chilled?" he added, his arms going around her.

"A little," she admitted, leaning back against him. "I should see to her accommodations, but I'd rather stay just where I am."

Acton turned her in his arms, and fiercely kissed her. "I'll warm you up," he murmured, and kissed her again.

"You abominable creature," she chuckled, putting her arms around his neck. "Have you no notions of propriety?"

"None whatever," he said, his lips once again on hers. "Damnation," he muttered, releasing her as a tap sounded on the door.

Jessica turned to smile at Saunders rolling in the tea cart. "How very good it looks," she said. "Do come and sit down, Acton. I'm quite famished. Why, Saunders. Red raspberries? I will certainly have a serving. And coconut cake? Really, Saunders, you will make me quite fat."

"I am happy your Grace is pleased," the butler said, giving her one of his rare smiles.

"Thank you. I am," she replied warmly, taking a seat beside the fire. "Oh, and Saunders. We passed her Grace, the Dowager Duchess, on the way here. Will you please have the rose chamber made ready for her. You may expect her arrival in something over an hour."

"I will see to it, your Grace," he bowed, and left the room.

"Quite starving, my dear," Acton murmured, taking the chair on the other side of the fire. "I fear I neglected to feed you."

"Indeed, you did. But no matter. This will do nicely. Acton, how do you know Grandmama will not make an extended visit?"

"If she were making one, several coaches would have followed along behind her. You would be astounded, my dear, at what Grandmama considers necessary for a lengthy stay."

"As much as that?" she chuckled, taking a sip of scalding tea.

"Only her entire wardrobe, plus the bulk of her furnishings, not to mention the majority of her servants."

"But where would we put it all?" she asked, eyes round.

"Simple, my dear. We'd merely remove everything from her rooms, and store it in the attics."

"The battle royal below stairs must assume epic proportions," Jessica laughed.

"Rest assured it does. I will never forget the last such occasion. I was sure Grandmama's dresser would come to blows with my valet. Each claimed seniority over the other."

"Who won?" she asked curiously, refilling his cup and returning it to him.

"I found it expedient to absent myself for a few days, taking Chollars with me, of course."

"Coward," she murmured.

"I thought it a stroke of genius. You know, my dear," he added, preparing to repay her in kind. "If you eat much more of that cake, you *will* become fat."

"What an unhandsome thing to say," she replied, helping herself to a further slice. "I should suppose that having a female fainting from hunger on your hands would be vastly distasteful to you."

"It would," he said, looking at her in amusement. "I have yet to discover any trace of the shrinking violet in you."

Laughter bubbled up in Jessica. "It would drive you to distraction if you did."

He studied her over the rim of his cup. "I should have taken you in hand before now. Well, no matter. All in good time. Grandmama's groom should shortly be blowing up the house."

Jessica looked startled. "Blowing up the house?" she repeated stupidly.

"On the yard of tin. What better way to announce one's imminent arrival, my dear? We will appear out front to greet her. On cue." He paused, and turned his head as a horn sounded in the distance. "From the sounds of it, I'll wager her coach has just turned into the avenue."

Jessica got up and crossed to the door. "Do I stand

beside you or in front of you?" she asked as she passed through the door.

"Behind me," he grinned, and went with her out front, wishing Grandmama elsewhere for the first time in his life.

CHAPTER XIII

"Eurice," said Grandmama, setting down her cup, "may be subject to the most alarming irritation of the nerves, but in this instance at least she made a good deal of sense. You have made a rare mull of it, between the two of you."

"Now, Grandmama," Acton said in soothing tones. "I know the journey here has tired you—"

An expression of disdain crossed her face. "I am made of sterner stuff. You needn't think to fob me off, my boy. What possessed you to run off in this imprudent fashion, I cannot imagine. Heaven only knows how many functions you had engaged to attend."

"I sent around our regrets," he said, goaded.

"Very commendable," Grandmama replied dryly. "It is absurd to think that your own departure hot on the heels of ordering McClean from town will go unnoticed."

Acton, who had picked up the decanter, and was in the act of pouring out a glass, looked across at her quickly. "How did you hear of that?" he asked curtly.

"If the intelligence I met with is at all correct, McClean made sure everyone heard of it. Not that that signifies—no one will pay much heed to him. Eurice may be a fool—in fact, I seldom make head or tail of what she says—but she can sometimes put what she wishes to say in a rational way."

Jessica flushed. "What did she tell you?" she said stiffly.

"I cannot conceive what possessed you, Jessica. Am I right in assuming that you went off with Wardly to unnerve Acton?"

"I'm afraid so," Jessica admitted almost inaudibly.

"I have considerable regard for you both, and want to see you happy. You shouldn't need me to tell you this is not the way to go about it, but that is your own affair. I am here to lend you countenance."

Acton regarded her with frank appraisal. "You are?" he said without the least sign of surprise.

Grandmama chuckled. "It may interest you to know that Mr. Wardly escorted Jessica here at my request."

Acton's chuckle answered hers. "May I inquire after my own whereabouts?"

"You drove down the previous afternoon to see to matters on the home farm. I should imagine you have seen to them by now."

"I hesitate to ask—you did include yourself in this Banbury tale?"

"Perhaps I should tell you that you knew of my intent to give Jessica my personal jewelry. I found it convenient—"

"No!" Jessica gasped. "I could never let you!"

"I found it convenient," Grandmama went on, ignoring the outburst, "to do so on my way to visit a friend. Lady Tolson, as you know, lives on the other side of Queensbridge."

"Grandmama," Jessica said with a great deal of asperity, "I am not so poor-spirited as to allow you to sacrifice—"

"Be quiet, child," Grandmama interrupted firmly. "You cannot stop me. My jewelry is mine to do with as I please. I should hate for McClean to get his hands on it. He would only gamble it away."

"If Grandmama wishes you to have it, Jessica, you will accept it," Acton said flatly.

"I'm sure she will," Grandmama said calmly. "Can you think of a better way to take Eurice's mind off the two of you? By now, she will have forgotten everything but my own duplicity."

"You do not appear to feel apprehensive about what she may say of you," Jessica murmured, mortified.

"Any silly creature who could be induced to heed Eurice is not of the least consequence," Grandmama replied, rising. "It is time I sought the comfort of my bed. I trust you will be able to restrain your wife while I rest, Acton."

"I will do my best," he promised, grinning, and crossed to hold the door open.

Until this humiliating moment, Jessica had never considered the far-reaching effects of her foolish pranks. With a clarity born of Grandmama's intervention, she viewed her behaviour through the eyes of others, and came up wanting. She knew quite well how she must appear.

"Do not let it vex you," Acton said when she had remained silent for several minutes.

She did not realize at first that he had spoken, for she had been lost in her own thoughts. "I'm sorry," she said, with a hollow laugh. "I'm afraid I was not attending."

"I said don't let it vex you," he repeated patiently.

"Grandmama has in her possession family jewels which I have never requested she hand over. They should rightfully now be in your possession."

"That is no great matter. I wasn't thinking of the jewelry."

He hesitated, and after a moment, said, "Surely you aren't subjecting yourself to the blue devils, Jessica. You do somewhat crazy things at times, but since I find them amusing, you should too."

"Crazy! You have hit on the very word. How clever of you."

"Oh, for God's sake! Go put on a habit. A good gallop should clear the cobwebs from your brain."

She found herself not proof against this inducement, and went swiftly upstairs to change. By the time she arrived out front, Acton was waiting to toss her up into the saddle. A gleam appeared in Jessica's eyes. Gathering up the reins, she lightly touched Lottie's flanks, and flew down the drive. Acton easily drew up beside her, and gave Beelzebub the office to pull ahead, but the stallion stubbornly maintained position. "You black-hearted limb of Satan," he growled under his breath. "I didn't bring you here to service that mare."

So it was that Jessica arrived at the end of the drive the winner. One glance at Acton was enough to bring a look of unholy glee to her face. "It would seem," she remarked smugly, "the male is ever the loser."

Acton refrained from comment, though with an effort. They took the north road, following along its twisting way, riding side by side until the rutted tracks forced him to ride behind. His eyes rested on her back, enjoying the sight of her slim body sitting so small and erect on the large mare, and he smiled at her when she turned to glance back at him. Coming to a crossroads, she drew Lottie to a halt and waited for him to ride up beside her. "Where do these roads lead?" she asked.

"I have no idea. Shall we take one?"

"The right. No—the left."

Acton threw back his head and laughed joyously. Jessica found herself laughing with him. Turning to the left, seemingly alone in the world, they rode along the pretty road hemmed in by high hedges. Rounding a curve they saw a cottage sitting in its beds of flowers, and waved to a woman in the yard, and chuckled at the squawking hens running from the horses' hooves.

To their right they glimpsed the sea, smooth and sparkling, and stretching in unbroken blue to lose itself in distant haze. At another fork in the road they saw a sign. "Addieborough," Jessica exclaimed. "It sounds interesting. Shall we take this turning?"

"Why not?" he answered, charmed by her ingenuous delight.

They came to the tiny village and wound along its twisting lanes lined with stone cottages basking in the sunlight. Dismounting at the local inn, they smiled at the children gathering to stare, and passed inside. A long bar stretched the length of the common room, one-third of it reserved for the local men, one-third for local couples, with the other third intended for visitors from other localities. Scattered along the other wall were small tables and chairs, slightly scarred and ancient in appearance. Guiding Jessica to a table, Acton seated her, and turned to the proprietor. "We are hoping you will furnish us with lunch," he said.

"I'll do my best, Governor. Though we don't have nothing fancy, you understand."

"Anything will do, I'm sure."

"The Missus can fix you a sandwich," the proprietor tentatively suggested.

Turning to Jessica, Acton said, "What is your preference, my dear?"

Turning red in the face, the landlord stammered, "Ham's all we got, Governor."

"Then bring two, please. And your best beer."

Jessica gazed about the room with interest. Catching the glance of two customers surreptitiously eyeing them, she smiled, receiving a shy bobbing of heads in reply. They found the sandwiches to be surprisingly good, with tender ham wedged between thick slices of buttered, homemade bread. Acton explained to Jessica that the beer companies were more particular in their selection of the proprietor's wife than in the qualities of the innkeeper himself, as she would be the cook. Approaching their table with a pitcher of beer, the landlord said, "The Missus made trifle this morning."

"Then by all means, bring two servings," Acton instantly agreed.

"Her trifle be surpassing good," one of the customers down the bar added helpfully.

Turning to the speaker, Acton remarked: "If it compares with the sandwiches, I am certain of it."

"Ye be strangers here," the man continued, interested.

"Yes, we are, and we find your countryside pleasing."

This slight encouragement was all the two inquisitive bystanders needed. Moving down the bar to perch on stools closer to Jessica and Acton, they smiled hopefully. "Where be ye from?" the spokesman asked.

"Over by Aynesworth," Acton replied vaguely.

"I never been over there," he was solemnly told.

"You would like our area, I think," Acton said affably, amused by their eagerness to gossip.

" 'Tis nice to meet folk from away," the second man offered.

"Indeed, it is. By the way, my name is John Alastair, and this is my wife."

"Glad to meet you," they chorused, bobbing their heads. The first speaker continued. "I be Jack Sill, and me friend here, he be Will Sykes. Are you going anywheres in particular?"

"No. We are just rambling about. Tell me, is there a local site we should visit?"

The two were doubtful. "Don't know as there's much," one of them replied. "Unless ye be interested in a ruin."

"A ruin!" Jessica exclaimed.

"As you see, we are," Acton chuckled.

"It be all tumbled down, like." The man called Jack seemed doubtful.

"All the more interesting," Acton returned, smiling at Jessica's eager face.

"Well, now, ye go on down past the church to the second turning, then ye go right—about a mile, I'd guess—and ye'll likely see it."

"They do say it be haunted," the man called Will offered.

"Haunted!" Jessica breathed, enthralled.

Acton threw up his hands in mock despair. "Then by all means, we must visit your ruin."

"Who haunts it?" Jessica demanded.

"They do say it be the monks. Though I never seen one myself."

"Squire did, though. Told me so hisself," Will solemnly added.

"Then it was a monastery?" Acton asked.

"Yes, that be so," Jack agreed. "Been a long time ago, though. Squire do say it be a ruin from the time of 'Enry."

"Squire do say it were torn down by 'Enry's soljers," Will added.

Following the directions supplied by Jack, they did indeed see the ruin in the distance. Built close to the sea, the monastery would at one time have housed a large order of monks, but in its present state it resembled nothing so much as a pile of stones tumbled in wild disarray, and overgrown with weeds. As they rode closer, the ruin took on alarming proportions. Some few sections of wall appeared to have survived the ravages of man and nature.

Picking their way among large stones and debris scattered about on the ground, they approached what would have been the entrance to the monastery. The gaping hole still had some of its supporting stones in place but the area just beyond was piled high with litter, some of it of recent origin, for wrapping papers blown about by the breeze gave evidence of its use by pleasure seekers enjoying a picnic lunch. They circled around the pile and approached from the rear, to find a more promising vista for exploration. Dismounting and tying the horses' reins to a clump of furze, they picked their way to the remains of a former passageway. "It appears to have been a connecting hall," Jessica remarked, peeping in. "Look, Acton. Rooms were along both sides. They must have been quite small."

"The monks' cells, I should imagine."

"I wonder what became of them."

"Some would have escaped, but many would have been imprisoned or disposed of in some manner. Those were harsh times, my dear."

Clambering over piles of stones, she peered into a dark opening leading downward into the ground. "Acton," she called. "See what I have found."

"Come away from there," he said, forcing the fear

from his voice as he walked up to her. "You run easily into danger. You have no idea what could be at the bottom of that hole. It could have been a well, or it could drop to a cellar floor many feet below. I can't turn my back—"

"I'm sorry," she gulped, chastised for once.

"I know," he answered, pulling her into his arms. "It is just that you sometimes frighten me."

Blushing, she glanced away. "I'm sorry," she whispered, stricken.

Acton's temper flared. "Don't keep saying you're sorry!" he snapped before he stopped to think.

"Very well, then," she snapped back. "I'm not sorry."

Acton suddenly chuckled, and kissed her, a very thorough kiss. "I see I must turn my mind to the taming of my pretty shrew."

"You may find the task beyond your powers," she told him, a complaisant look on her face.

A muscle jerking in his jaw, he regretfully took his arms from about her, and led her to the horses. After tightening the girths, he took her foot between his hands and threw her up into the saddle. Jessica accepted the reins he handed her and settled herself as he swung into his own saddle. It was by now late afternoon. They rode over the hills and descended into a valley, pausing at last beside a gushing stream.

"Do let us have a drink," she urged, mischief in her face as she slid to the ground. Cupping her hands to sip the cold water, she glanced at Acton in the act of lifting a drink to his lips, and flicked droplets at his face. Turning his eyes in her direction, he was just in time to receive a handful in the face. Laughing merrily, she evaded his lunge and scurried up the bank, only to be caught before she had taken a dozen steps.

"So you would tease," he chuckled, his leg sweeping her feet from beneath her and dropping her to the ground. His body cushioned the fall and he held her tightly as his lips swooped on hers, and they rolled over on the ground. Caught up in sudden passion, he failed to realize the danger, and the next instant they had tumbled down the bank and into the stream.

Jessica came to a sitting position in the water, shivering with the cold. "Well!" she exclaimed indignantly. "Of all the nitwitted things to do!"

Acton threw back his head and laughed. "If you could see yourself," he gasped, eyeing the feather on her hat, now sodden and drooping forlornly forward over her brow.

"How fortunate it is you look so neat yourself," she shot back, struggling to her feet, and attempting to hold her dripping skirts away from her body. "I should think the least you could do would be to give me a hand."

Turning away, she sloshed her way out of the stream. She had the start on him as she struggled up the bank, but he caught up with her by the time she arrived beside the horses. Placing his sodden jacket about her shoulders, he said, "Perhaps it will afford you some warmth. I'm sorry, Jessica."

Her voice, when it came from between her chattering teeth, was unsteady. "Pray say no more about it," she muttered, and allowed him to help her to mount, while Lottie danced about on nervous hooves, made uncomfortable by the feel of cold skirts clinging to her flanks.

"We will soon have you home," he replied, mounting Beelzebub. "A hot bath—watch out for rabbit holes," he called after her as she set Lottie forward into a gallop.

He soon overtook her, and tore homeward beside her, Beelzebub, surefooted, guiding the excited mare safely onward. By the time they reached Aynesworth, Jessica was numb with cold, her mind drained of all thought other than the necessity of clinging to Lottie's back. Arrived before the door, she tumbled into Acton's waiting arms, and sagged half-sobbing against his chest. He rushed inside with her, and up the stairs, issuing orders in rapid succession to the gaping servants. In spite of her misery, Jessica could not help but be amused by the way they scurried before him, for all the world like so many ants whose hill had been disturbed.

Twenty minutes later, stripped of her sodden clothing, she lay luxuriating in a hot bath, the warmth chasing away the chill. Unaware that Acton had entered and stood watching, she raised one leg, dribbling water over it with the sponge. His eyes devoured the sight of her wet skin glowing in the candlelight, and he caught his breath when she sat upright, exposing her breasts to view. Jessica, hearing the slight sound, turned her head, and gasped. "What are you doing here?" she demanded, suddenly shy, and sinking into the tub until the water rose about her shoulders.

"I came to check on you," he remarked, crossing to stand looking down at her. "You are a fetching sight, my sweet," he added, chuckling softly, and plucked the sponge from her nerveless fingers.

Jessica came alive. "What are you doing? Give that back," she said, holding out a hand.

"What am I doing? Why, bathing you, of course."

"Of all the ridiculous starts!" she exclaimed. "I am quite capable of doing it myself."

"But I am an experienced handmaiden, my dear," he remarked in silken tones.

"So you admit it, do you? No doubt you learned it from your—well, never mind. How you can have the effrontery—"

"How can you have the impropriety, my sweet, to betray your understanding of things you should know nothing about?" he shot back provocatively, reaching out a hand to caress her skin.

A curl dropping onto a shoulder from the mass pinned high atop her head caught her notice. As she raised her arms to tuck it back in place, her breasts thrust upward, rosy and bouncing. "You're tempting fate," Acton remarked, his eyes feasting on the sight.

Jessica quickly lowered her arms and reached for the soap, but his hand grasped it first. "Relax, and enjoy it," he said, lathering the sponge. Kneeling beside the tub, he gently washed her arms and shoulders, and moved on downward, paying particular attention to her breasts. "Thank you," she said somewhat breathlessly. "I will be able to continue now."

"I make it a rule never to leave a task partially undone," he said, moving on downward over her stomach, and on downward still. "I am most happy to assist you," he added, his hand brushing caressingly over her thighs.

Jessica giggled. "Remember my bath, sir," she said teasingly.

He raised his gaze to her face. "You make it difficult for me to remember anything, sweet," he said. Lifting her from the tub, he wrapped her in a towel, and patted her dry. Tossing the towel aside, he pulled her soft curves against his hard body, and sought her lips. Lifting her in his arms, he carried her to her bedroom, and the bed.

"What of your honour?" she asked softly.

"The devil with my honour," he murmured huskily as he laid her gently down.

Jessica languidly watched him shrug out of his robe, and trembled, thinking of all the useless scheming she had done in hopes of bringing about such a scene as this. One rapid movement and she was engulfed in his embrace, his mouth on hers in a drugging kiss of passion. Almost immediately he was over her, his lips trailing over her throat to her breasts, until, no longer able to contain himself, he took her with him to the heights of ecstasy. Their passions sated, he cradled her in his arms, clasped her close against his side. "Jessie, Jessie," he murmured, his lips pressing little nibbling kisses over her face. "I was wrong. So wrong. I should never let my foolish pride keep us from this."

"I trust you are now prepared to reform your ways," she smiled, tracing a finger around his lips.

He smoothed the hair from her brow, and chuckled. "When I catch my breath, dear love, you will have no doubts of that."

A breeze moving the curtains at the windows the following morning played softly over the pair entwined in sleep within the bed, bringing with it first a hint of rain and finally the faint sound of thunder rumbling in the distance. Jessica stirred and opened her eyes, a dreamy half-smile curving her lips. Turning her cheek to rest against his shoulder, she trailed her fingers over his chest and around a masculine nipple, caressing it lightly, until his hand shot out to grasp her wrist. "Take care, my sweet," his voice murmured lazily from above her head. "You just might rouse the sleeping beast."

" 'Tis time he woke. It seems a shame to waste the day."

His shoulders began to shake. "Do but recollect, my pet. He is entitled to his rest."

"Ungrateful brute," she said lovingly. "What are you thinking?"

"That you look enticing."

"Are you enticed?"

"Yes," he murmured, kissing her lingeringly. "By the siren I married one day."

Jessica sighed in contentment. "Do you know, Acton," she mused thoughtfully, "you must have your portrait painted. I will hang it just there, facing the bed," she added, pointing. "I will always think of you when I see it."

"You will not need a picture to think of me," he grinned. "I plan to be about."

She giggled, and melted within his arms. "Acton," she began.

"Shh, sweet," he admonished, continuing with his kisses.

"I was just wondering—"

He lifted his head, and stared into her eyes. "Jessica, I have been without you for weeks. I have been hard pressed, but no longer. Now, be quiet," he added, bending hungrily over her.

CHAPTER XIV

A tap sounding on the door was followed immediately by the entrance of Saunders, announcing the arrival of General Bainbridge. That gentleman came in and crossed to raise Grandmama's fingers to his lips. "Well, Clementine," he said jovially. "You are looking well, I'm happy to see."

"What a pleasant surprise," she said, laying aside her book. "What brings you here, Ernest?"

"I had ridden to these parts on business and met with the tidings that you were here. I was profoundly shocked not to have known of it."

"I am here for a short time only. I am not so foolish as to move in with my grandson, I promise you. The young cannot be expected to countenance having an oldster always under foot. I stopped off on my way to visit Edna Tolson. I shan't linger at Aynesworth past tomorrow."

"You cannot mean you are wandering over the countryside alone," he said, much struck. "It isn't safe, you know."

"My coachman and groom carry firearms. You have known me for too many years, Ernest, to suppose me faint hearted."

"I confess to some fear for the safety of any scoundrel foolish enough to accost you," the General said with a smile. "However, Clementine, I see my duty clear. It will be my pleasure to escort you the remainder of your journey."

Grandmama had crossed to the bellpull to ring for refreshments, but she turned toward him upon hearing this statement. The gleam of amusement in her eyes became pronounced. "No one would conceivably wish to accost me," she said, and pulled the bell.

"I would," he replied, twinkling. "For my part, I always thought the Duke a lucky devil."

The arrival of the tea cart coincided with that of Acton. He came striding into the room, but checked his step upon perceiving the General. Recovering himself, he moved forward and held out his hand. "This is well thought of, sir," he said, smiling.

"I know you were not expecting me, my boy. You must allow me to apologize."

"Do not, I beg you. May I offer you some wine?"

An expression of acute regret crossed the General's face. "I say yes, but my doctor says no," he admitted ruefully.

"Pray do not tell me you allow that to deter you," Grandmama said in disbelief. "Regardless of what you would have your doctor think, I do not believe it."

"Well, and I should hope not," he retorted, unruffled. "I will have a Scotch, Acton, if I may."

Acton, who had resumed his seat, rose and crossed to give the order to a footman. "May I say, sir, that I hope we are not abetting you in an action that will damage your health."

"At our age, my boy, we take our pleasures where we find them. Eh, Clementine?"

She chuckled and went on to speak of other matters, eventually telling Acton of the General's intention to escort her to Lady Tolson's. Acton, objecting, said he had meant doing so himself, and objected further when she announced she was leaving on the morrow; but Grandmama remained adamant.

Jessica, when told, could appreciate her feelings. She herself would not relish being the extra person present. On the following morning, she went out front with Acton to bid Grandmama a fond farewell. Left to her own devices when he later closeted himself with his secretary, she placed a shawl about her shoulders and went outside to stroll for a time in the gardens. Tiring of this activity, she returned to the house and went to her rooms. The first sight that met her eyes was Grandmama's jewel casket spank in the middle of her bed. "Oh!" she stormed on perceiving its contents. Slamming the lid down, she turned on her heel and rushed downstairs. William, the groom on duty in the hall below, was far too well trained to display emotion, but he was very conscious of the stormy expression on her Grace's face. Crossing to hold open the door to the library, he bowed respectfully as she passed within, and regretfully closed it. He would very much have liked leaving it ajar in hopes of overhearing what was about to transpire within the room. His curiosity was to remain unsatisfied.

Some ten minutes were to elapse before the door reopened, and their Graces emerged. William allowed himself one quick glance at her Grace's face, through the simple expedient of turning toward them as if awaiting instructions, noting in so doing that her expression had moderated, and was now, in fact, quite pleasant. Given orders from his Grace to send word to the stables to have Lottie and Beelzebub out front in thirty minutes, William bowed, and went off to comply.

CHAPTER XV

Acton had been in a most pleasant mood as they leisurely traversed narrow lanes and open fields, and rode along ancient stone fencing until they came to the sea. Dismounted, they watched the wheeling of gulls and waded in the shallows before pausing to partake of a picnic lunch, their backs resting against the rocks. Wild creatures scurried about in sparse grasses nearby, and sheep grazed in the distance as clouds formed and reformed over the hills. Quite suddenly, it seemed, the sky took on an ominous look. Jessica could not but be aware of the gravity of Acton's face as he led her to the mare and tossed her up into the saddle. "You will be drenched," he said sternly in a voice very different from the bantering tones he had hitherto employed.

"I have been wet before," she said saucily. "Why, every time I take a bath—"

"I trust you will someday rid yourself of the habit of blurting out whatever comes into your head," he said in his dryest tones as he swung up into his saddle.

Jessica obediently hung her head, but he could not

think her in any wise chastened. "I don't know what takes such strong possession of my mind at times that I speak before I think," she murmured provocatively. "I expect that I am wanton."

Acton, worried about the weather, allowed the remark to pass, looking around instead for some means of sheltering her from the storm. Seeing a cottage in the distance, he leaned forward to grasp her bridle and urge the horses forward. They found the dwelling a ruin, with one wall caved in and thatch hanging drunkenly from those remaining. Although the lean-to attached to one side had faired little better than the house, he led the horses under the scant cover it provided, rubbed them down, and pulled what forage he could find within their reach before dashing inside to join Jessica.

Together they surveyed their haven, for haven it was, however rude and dirty. "Well," she said. "At least it is dry."

Acton satisfied himself that no unwanted creatures kept them company, and spread his coat upon the floor. "If Madam wishes," he grinned. "Her pallet awaits."

Jessica stared. "Surely you don't intend making love in this place," she said in some surprise.

"In this place, or any place, my love."

Her eyes moved downward along his lean frame to the bulge now evident. Yes, she knew, he did intend. Suddenly she blushed: it seemed so brazen somehow, in the daytime, amid such surroundings.

" 'Twill be more comfortable lying down," he remarked pleasantly. "But if you prefer to stand—"

Jessica retreated a cautious step, trying to concentrate her mind. The thought of expected guests steadied her. "Your sister is due to arrive," she said, clutching at straws. "We must not tarry—"

"Don't bring yourself into a pet, for it is not of the least consequence. Emaline has yet to be on time." He was holding out his hand, a hint of impatience in his attitude which Jessica thought it wise not to test.

He was in no hurry—leisurely his hands moved over her with a thoroughness that left her blushing. Never had she felt so naked. A thought occurred to her. "You're treating me like a mistress," she said tartly.

"Every man should have a mistress. When he has wife and lover in one small body, he is the luckiest of men."

"You insult me," she shot back sharply.

"Quite the contrary, my dear. I compliment you. Not every woman can satisfy both sides of her man's nature."

"And if there is another side to mine?" she demanded. "What then?"

"I will be both husband and servicer," came his bland reply.

"Oh," stormed Jessica. "Of all the egotistical—"

"Gently, my own. Gently. You have yet to learn the full, sweet range of love." Lifting his head, he smiled into her eyes. "Not many ladies are so fortunate in their choice of tutor."

"And what of your student?" she asked, a twinkle coming into her eyes.

"I am content."

"I hope that Jimminy Cricket is also," she chortled as his eyes flew wide.

Meanwhile, back at Aynesworth, his Grace's sister was frankly worried. As fair of skin as he was dark, she shared the same classic profile and deep blue eyes inherited from their father, but while Acton's lips were as arched as hers, there was a sweetness of expression about Lady Emaline's mouth that was generally held to have come to her through their mother. At present that mouth trembled as if its owner would dissolve into tears upon her brother's hearth rug. "I vow, Austin, you should send someone to look for them!" she exclaimed to her husband in pleading tones. " 'Tis past six of the clock, and they have not returned."

"I send for them! Indeed not! Acton wouldn't like it, and I couldn't blame him, I might add."

Emaline, casting a pained look in his direction, paid scant attention to this craven speech. "Heaven knows I would never urge you to do anything you found distasteful," she stated with supreme disregard for past instances of a similar nature, "but it is high time you bestirred yourself. How you can just sit there, while I live in hourly dread—"

"Now, my dear," protested her lord, a gentleman long inured to such vagaries from his beloved.

"—of John being brought home on a door," she finished in triumph. "He is so scatterbrained, you know."

"Scatterbrained!" Lord Marrivane ejaculated, stunned. "I have never heard such a farrago as that. A more self-contained, determined man than Acton, I have yet to meet."

"You will allow me, Austin, a certain understanding of my own brother, I should think," said her ladyship with a great deal of resolution.

"Well, my dear, if that is a sample of your understanding," his lordship shot back, "you are far and away wide of the mark."

Lady Emaline's intention of calling on heaven as a witness to the truth of her protestations was forestalled by a familiar voice drawling from the doorway. "I appear the subject of some dispute, it seems."

"John!" Emaline gasped, a quantity of disordered locks tumbling about her shoulders as she rushed across the room to hurl herself into his arms.

"Exactly," he murmured, bestowing a brotherly peck upon her cheek. "You were ever a surprise, my dear. On time this once, I perceive."

"And is that my new sister?" Emaline asked, enfolding Jessica in a soft embrace. "But she is adorable, John. I just know we will positively dote on one another."

Acton broke into a laugh. "Jessica, as you may have surmised, this impulsive creature is my sister. And you must meet Austin, my brother-in-law."

"Run along," said Emaline as Lord Marrivan raised Jessica's fingers to his lips. "Jessica and I have much to discuss. I want to hear how you met, and all about your wedding, and—oh, just everything. We regretted not having been present," she continued, pulling Jessica somewhat tempestuously to a settee, "but I was just in my third confinement, you apprehend, and dear Austin simply would not hear of travel until I had delivered. But we are fortunate, in any event," she rattled on, much to the relief of Jessica, for she did not look forward to questions concerning her meeting with Acton. "The wet nurse is quite presentable," Emaline was saying, "so we could leave dear, darling little Helene with the utmost confidence. Though I will admit our other two children seem prone to land themselves in the most impossible starts of mischief."

"I am anxious to see them," Jessica managed into the pause that followed Emaline's discourse.

"You must visit us at your earliest opportunity. For they and we, the children, I mean, cannot all travel here, the children being such babies, you understand."

"I hesitate to intrude, my dears," Acton said, coming over to them. "But if we are to dress for dinner, we had best repair to our rooms."

Emaline, rising, said, "Jessica and I have become most happily acquainted. Have we not, dearest sister?"

"Most happily," Jessica agreed, while feeling somewhat overwhelmed.

When she entered the drawing room almost an hour later, Jessica was able to greet the others with at least the appearance of composure. But it was not easy, she found, to reply to Emaline's questions of the wedding without expecting a further query regarding the circumstances of her first meeting with Acton. By the time they sat down to dinner she was ready to admit all. She had not long to reflect on what she would say, however, for Saunders had scarcely served the soup before Emaline remarked, "You haven't told us how you met."

Into the silence that followed, Jessica suddenly spoke. "We may as well tell them, Acton," she said, smiling rather dolefully.

"As you wish, my dear. But later."

"You need tell us nothing," Emaline said, seeing the look that passed between them. "You are fortunate indeed, John, to have acquired a superlative cook. If we do not improve the product from our kitchens, I vow Austin will take his meals away from home."

"You cannot conceive what I am forced to swallow," Austin agreed. "You may well find this visit protracting itself," he added, attacking with gusto each course placed before him. "Were I to die tonight," he sighed at the conclusion of the meal, "I would go happy."

"Where you are going," said Emaline, "is to the drawing room with Jessica and me."

"Where you are going, my dear, is to bed," contradicted Austin. "You are not long past your latest confinement, remember."

"How dull," she protested, pouting prettily. But she immediately rose, said her good-nights, and allowed Austin to escort her from the room.

Jessica waited until they were out of earshot before catching Acton's eye. "What will we tell them if they again ask how we met?"

"Not we, sweet. I will tell them in private."

"I would not be embarrassed—"

"I owe you that much, at the least. To have put you in the position of marrying a stranger—"

"But you didn't seem a stranger, Acton. Do you ever wonder if we could have known one another in —another life?"

Grinning, he walked around the table to assist her from her chair. "At the moment, I am only interested in knowing you in this life," he said with a glint in his eye she could not miss. "And now you too, my dear, are going up to bed."

It was at breakfast the following morning that Acton suggested a fishing expedition. Jessica, in the act of conveying a bit of egg to her mouth, paused with the fork suspended in midair. "Fishing?" she said in stupified tones.

"Good Lord!" breathed Emaline, laying down her cutlery. "Really, John. Of all the birdbrained—"

"We will take a lunch," he declared with what the ladies could only consider vulgar enthusiasm. "Finish your breakfast. We will want an early start."

"You men may fish if you feel you must," Emaline said in reasonable tones. "Jessica and I will find other pursuits to occupy our time."

"Nonsense, my dear," Austin protested. "Of course you will join us. The exercise will do you a world of good."

"But, Acton," Jessica began. "If Emaline—"

"Our minds are made up. Eh, Austin?"

"But I do not possess a wardrobe for such revolting pastimes," Emaline offered by way of objection. "I doubt not Jessica—"

"You will find something, my dear," Austin informed her dryly.

She stared first at him and then at Jessica. "Whatever does one wear to fish?" she asked, honestly puzzled.

"I have no idea," Jessica replied, equally at sea.

"Just put on something pretty," Acton remarked, consulting his watch. "And do hurry."

The gentlemen were surprised by the vision their somewhat rebellious wives presented as they emerged from the house, for they had donned frivolous muslin gowns, with lace mittens covering their hands. Opening frilly parasols, they held them jauntily above their heads as they came tripping down the steps.

"I must have misunderstood," Austin told Acton, eyeing them grimly. "I thought you said fishing. I didn't realize we were attending a tea party."

"How do you expect to ride in those—rig-outs?" Acton demanded.

"Does one ride when one fishes?" Emaline inquired innocently.

"Go in and change," said Austin.

"Why, gentlemen," Jessica smiled sweetly. "We thought we had put on something pretty."

Suddenly grinning, Acton capitulated. "We are overset, Austin, and must concede the point. Bring around the carriage, Jenks."

When it had arrived, and Acton had settled into his seat facing the ladies, Austin looked at him with resignation. "When you have been married as long as I, you will learn to avoid concessions whenever possible," he said from the heart.

Jessica sat watching the scenery with interest as they rolled on along the sun-dappled road. The carriage drawing to a halt made her recollect her surroundings. "Why are we stopping?" she asked, looking about in bewilderment. "I don't see any water."

"There is no road to the stream," Acton blandly replied, reaching out a hand to assist her to the ground.

Jessica ignored the gleam in his eye, considering it safer to do so, which indeed it was, since Acton only wanted the opportunity to say something outrageous. With a great deal of resolution she set off across the field and stumbled over the rough ground, but stubbornly held the parasol above her head. They were obliged to follow along the bank of the winding stream, a circumstance which caused her slippers to become quite wet, and by the time Acton declared that they had reached the ideal spot for their sport, she had accepted, if ruefully, the humour of it all.

Spreading a blanket under a tree, Acton said, "You may wish to rest while we prepare the lines."

"I have ever valued you as my dearest brother, John," Emaline declared, "but I will not touch that—whatever it is."

"Now, Emaline—"

"Never!"

Having received this put-down with perfect equanimity, Acton joined Austin to set about the all-absorbing business of digging for worms. It was now considerably after eleven o'clock, and, although the sun shone brightly, a light breeze kept the air from becoming too warm. Settling down on the blanket, Jessica and Emaline watched them curiously until, when Acton paused to remove his coat and lay it on the bank, Jessica said, "Whatever do you suppose they can be doing?"

"I haven't any notion," Emaline replied. "It looks frightfully dirty, if you ask me."

A hush, except for the sound of water bubbling merrily over rounded stones lying in the bed of the stream, fell over the scene as the gentlemen, gazing in companionable silence at the fish lazily moving their fins in its depths, dangled baited hooks tantalizingly before their quarry. Emaline, who was busily engaged in smoothing her skirts to allay any wrinkling, paused in her efforts to remark, "I wonder what mischief my two oldest are up to at this moment. I vow I miss them prodigiously."

Jessica looked quickly across at her. "Of course you must."

"Well, as to that, nothing could have kept me away. I did so want to meet you, dearest sister, but you will know I shan't stay away from my babies for too terribly long. And I must say, I hope you will soon give Acton an heir. I simply cannot abide the thought of McClean's remaining so for one instant longer than is absolutely necessary."

Jessica, her gaze steadily on her, came to a decision. "I worry about McClean, Emaline. Oh, I know Acton believes him harmless, but McClean's expectations may mean more to him than anyone realizes. He did visit Aynesworth while Acton was away, I gathered for the express purpose of labelling me emotionally unstable. I feel sure he would like to eliminate me before I do bear Acton an heir."

Emaline uttered a faint shriek. "Does John know of this?" she demanded, horrified.

"I haven't told him, no," Jessica replied, with unruffled calm. "He would only take it into his head that he must watch over me day and night. And there is, after all, little harm McClean can do to me. It is what he might attempt against Acton that worries me."

"John is well able to take care of himself," Emaline replied, with less concern. She determined to take the first opportunity to relate Jessica's experience to Acton. She continued to chat of other matters for a time, then became drowsy in the warmth of the shade beneath the tree. The sound of the water moving over rocks and the whisper of leaves moving on a breeze had a lulling effect, and they drifted into sleep.

A bird singing overhead awakened Jessica. Glancing up, she saw Acton gazing down at her, his eyes tender. "Oh," she murmured, struggling to a sitting position. "Have you fished?"

Laughing, he held out a glistening string. "Aren't they beauties?" he said, beaming with pride.

"Ugh!" Emaline shuddered. "Take that revolting mess away this instant. You are dripping all over me."

Backing away, Acton glanced at Jessica. "They're lovely, dear," she smiled. "So—" She searched her mind. "—fresh," she produced.

"Just see mine!" Austin demanded, coming over to them with a string in his hand.

Jessica and Emaline exchanged a look. "Yes, dear. They are nice," Emaline said, finally.

"What do you plan to do with them?" Jessica asked curiously.

"Take them home, of course," Acton promptly replied.

"We will have them for breakfast," Austin added.

"Pray, do not tell me," Emaline said with surprise, "that you intend they ride in the carriage with us."

Acton chuckled, and said, "They will be on the seat with McCauley. Now, do let us eat. We are starving."

Jessica and Emaline ran their eyes rather sardonically over them. Both gentlemen had mud on their trousers and their feet were wet. A smear of dirt ran down Austin's cheek, and Acton's sleeve was torn. They resembled nothing so much as grubby, happy boys.

"We washed our hands in the stream," Acton explained rather sheepishly.

"Oh," said Jessica. "Well, it is always agreeable to have the problem of one's grooming solved."

CHAPTER XVI

His Grace was standing at a table in the library of Acton House with his back to the door, a sheaf of papers (which he did not appear to be reading) in his hand. His thoughts were filled with the implications of an announcement made by Emaline, regarding the latest of McClean's misdeeds. That Jessica viewed it with composure did little to allay his own alarm, for who could tell what his cousin might do? He was—yes, there was no use avoiding the truth— he was dangerous. There had been, next, the necessity of journeying to London to lay the facts before McClean. Face to face it must be; no other way would do. And then there was, thirdly, Acton's own insatiable longing for Jessica. He missed her in his bed, but he also missed her easy wit and joyous response to life. Depend on it, he mused, physical union was but one facet of a love such as theirs.

"You sent for me?" McClean's voice drawled from the doorway, interrupting his reverie.

Acton turned and surveyed him dispassionately.

"Come in, McClean," he said with controlled emotion.

McClean strolled across the room to stand by the fire. "Well, what is it now?" he said peevishly. "I really am short of time—"

"I think you will find our conversation illuminating," Acton said evenly.

"As to that—oh, very well," McClean began, put out but nevertheless taking the proffered chair across from Acton's desk. Shaking out the ruffles at his wrist, he congratulated himself on his appearance, gazing down with approval upon his red shoes.

Acton regarded him steadily. In earlier times he would have viewed his relative with tolerant amusement. Not so now. "I trust you are not considering your succession to my shoes," he observed dryly.

"Oh, no. Hardly that," McClean handsomely assured him.

"You relieve my mind."

"However, we must consider that possibility," McClean continued gravely. "One is regrettably not immortal."

"Very true, McClean. But I do not think you should build on that. I have some years still before me, I would think."

"In the course of nature, no doubt you do."

"I enjoy excellent health, would you not say?"

"Yes, true. You were ever fortunate in that respect. However, considering the nature of our relationship, you will admit I would be extremely remiss not to be concerned."

"I fail to take your meaning." Acton seemed puzzled. "Pray enlighten me."

"As your heir, I mean," McClean answered shortly.

"It is my denseness, to be sure," Acton smoothly explained. "You must bear with me, McClean, for I regret I am slow to comprehend."

"Now, don't mistake me, Alastair. You must not think your demise would bring me joy. I would feel a deep sense of bereavement, should you depart this life."

"Thank you," his Grace bowed slightly, his face showing little emotion.

"However," McClean went on, "you must allow me to look to the future, sad though this contemplation proves."

"Considering how uncertain is this life."

"I did not in the least mean—"

"I trust not," Acton remarked, sitting at his ease, his fingers toying with the ink stand on his desk. "Since you tell me so," he added gently, with something not quite pleasant gleaming deep within his eyes.

McClean flushed and looked away. "You may ridicule, but you were ever prone to accidents, you may recall." Upon turning his eyes again upon Acton, and seeing the surprised elevation of his Grace's brow, he concluded somewhat lamely, "I would certainly be negligent in my obligations, should I shrink from any responsibility I owe the family."

Acton surveyed him sardonically from beneath lowered lids. "This concern for your relations is something new, is it not?"

"Your humour is ill-timed, cousin. You will not find so amusing what I must disclose. Indeed, though my tidings are distressing, it falls to my painful lot to apprise you of my recent discovery."

"Your discourse is of course interesting, McClean," Acton said wearily, "despite your usual tendency to wander from the point."

Flushing, McClean laughed harshly. "I will overlook your levity at this time, for you are under stress. Yes, a very great stress, as is to be expected. It is with reluctance—yes, the most profound reluctance, I must repeat—that I find myself the bearer of ill tidings—indeed, tidings of the saddest sort—though you don't appear fully to appreciate—at least, my attention has been drawn—"

"McClean, your eloquence is no doubt a point of pride with you." Acton paused, ran his eye over him, and added dryly, "As is your dress. But I, too, have tidings to disclose. It will please me greatly if you will confine your remarks to those pertinent to the point you wish to make."

McClean swallowed his annoyance. "I had hoped to save you pain—"

"You need not trouble yourself unduly," Acton remarked during the pause that followed.

"Very well," McClean snapped. "As it is, and always has been, my custom not to pry—"

Acton raised speaking eyebrows, but remained silent.

"As I said," McClean stammered, "without seeking, but most regretfully finding, a certain conduct in your wife, I must now relate—"

Acton's eyes never wavered from his face, but McClean sensed a tension and briefly wondered at the advisability of his disclosures. "Yes, McClean?" Acton prompted, his voice silken. "A certain conduct in my wife?"

"Exactly," McClean plunged heedlessly on. "I only slowly recognized the implications, for her behaviour did not appear to be what I would have been led to expect. Indeed, I was shocked—yes, shocked, I say—at the instability of her emotional—"

He got no further, for Acton's hand slammed down hard on his desk as he leaned forward to grasp McClean's lapels. Dragging him half out of his chair, Acton, his eyes blazing, slapped him repeatedly with ferocity. His eyes bulging and his ears ringing from the blows, McClean was hurled back into the chair, from which he gazed at his cousin in abject fear.

"You lying, filthy cur," Acton spat. "You dare to speak so of my wife! I should kill you!" As McClean, trembling, attempted to sit upright, rubbing his hands against his face, Acton said, "and I will kill you if you ever speak of her so again." He continued with a quiet more deadly to McClean's ears than his shouting voice had ever been. "If you are wise, you will not repeat your lies abroad, for I will hear them and seek you out. Do you attend me?"

Trembling before the truth he read in Acton's face, McClean mutely nodded.

"I have been easy with you in the past. But no more. You will leave now—never to return."

"But—" McClean quavered.

"Never! Make no mistake about it." Crossing to the door, Acton spoke to Saunders. "Lord McClean is leaving. Send for his carriage. He will be denied admittance to all of my residences in future."

Saunders bowed, his face expressionless. "Certainly, your Grace," he said.

In the early hours of the following morning, in her dreams, Jessica heard Acton's voice. "Jessica," he was whispering, his lips touching hers. "Jessica!"

Struggling up from sleep, she murmured, "Acton? Oh, are you home? Good. I've been waiting to hear what happened in London."

"Not tonight." His eyes glinted wickedly into hers. "I have other plans for tonight."

When she awakened in the morning he was bending over her, his eyes lovingly studying her face. "You look like a little kitten," he murmured tenderly.

"A kitten!" she said, surprised.

"Well, not precisely, now I come to think of it. A jungle cat, perhaps?"

She smiled precociously. "I think," she said, "that you have the most fertile brain of anyone of my acquaintance. May I inquire what in particular you produced for McClean's benefit?"

"Rest assured McClean will never be a threat to you again. I could forgive him much, but his menace to you I will not tolerate."

She gazed up at him, her grey eyes wide. "You will not harm him?" she asked tremulously.

"No, though I would enjoy the pleasure." He took her hand in his large one, and raised it to his lips. "I have known since childhood that he was strange, but I did not want to believe him mad or dangerous. We played together as boys, and he was my heir. It is difficult to admit that a relative—"

"Yes, I know. Do not torture yourself, Acton."

"I have waited long for you, Jessica. I did not believe in love until I found you. Now that I have, I will never let you go."

CHAPTER XVII

McClean surveyed the man with repugnance, regretting the necessity for dealing with such loathsome scum. His fastidious nature rebelled at this close proximity to such a creature, but their association was unfortunately necessary if he was to realize a happy conclusion of his plans. "You've bungled from the start, you stupid fool," he growled menacingly.

"Lord luv yer honour, I got we winkers on 'er," the man whined. "But I ain't no common prig. I be a bridle cull, I be, workin' on a dancer, not in the way o' goin' without me barker."

"What in damnation is he talking about, Courtney?" McClean demanded of his flunkey.

"He says he is a highwayman, my lord, and accustomed to working with a horse and pistols."

"I'll get 'er, yer honour," the man assured McClean. "I keeps me nag at a flash ken I knows about. Bidin' me time, 'er'll be free o' the flash cove, and I kin snatch 'er."

"You fool!" McClean breathed. "What would I do with her? Answer me that!"

"Lord luv yer honour, I thought ye wanted 'er."

"Dead! Dead, do you hear!" McClean yelled, beside himself with rage.

"I don told ye 'is Grice be a rum go."

"Courtney," McClean said, struggling for control. "You said this man knew his business."

"He does, my Lord. But his Grace has become most particular in his protection of her Grace."

"That's the truth, yer honour," the highwayman broke in. "'Er has two coves aguardin' 'er when 'er rides out."

"Perhaps you will be so good as to inform me how you plan to contrive a satisfactory solution to this difficulty, provided you are capable of contemplation in any form."

"Eh?"

"Lord Alastair means," Courtney translated for the highwayman, "how will you get to her if she is well guarded."

"'E be a rare gager, don't 'e. Tell 'im I kin lay low 'till I clap me winkers on 'er again. I seen 'er down to the village not three days gone."

"What?" McClean gasped, jumping to his feet. "You saw her? Where?"

"She be havin' a spot o' tea, yer honour. With another 'un."

"Permit me, my lord," Courtney bowed. "I understand his Grace's sister and brother-in-law are presently guests at Aynesworth."

"Emaline."

"Precisely, my lord. Her Grace and her ladyship were no doubt visiting the tea room in the village."

"Then they will in all probability take the coach out again."

"Undoubtedly, my lord."

"Umm," McClean mused. "Perfect. It could not be better. You," he said, turning his gaze upon the highwayman. "You will wait until she again rides out in the coach. Do you understand? Make no attempt to kill her until she is in the coach!"

"Lord luv us," gasped the man. "The swell ain't likely to be about when the tattler's up."

"The moon, my lord," supplied Courtney.

"Good God!" McClean cried. "What has the moon to do with it?"

"I ain't lookin' to be nabbled, yer honour. Not fer no thin truss, I ain't."

"Courtney," McClean demanded.

"He does not wish to run the risk of arrest, my lord. At least, not for the sum he is to receive."

"Damn you," hissed McClean. "We had an agreement."

"I never worked the dayglim, yer honour. It be tricksey, it be."

"How much?" McClean growled, scowling.

"I be needin' ter use the flash ken o' some bridle culls I knows about. They work the 'Igh Toby, but they be friends. Thicken the truss, and they'll likely let me use it."

"How much, I say!"

"Twenty guineas fer each of 'em, yer honour."

"Oh, very well. Just kill her, you hear?"

"One thing more, yer honour. Coaches be tricksy rabblers, they be. I'd best lie low at me friends place till 'er rides out alone, yer honour. I don't got a fancy fer the dayglim, and sure not no guarded coach."

"I will leave the details to you. Just make sure it appears an ordinary holdup. Suspicion must not point to me."

The more he pondered, the more McClean was pleased with the developments. Murder during a holdup might not be so closely questioned, while a shooting on Aynesworth land most definitely would. The weakness in the latter plan lay in convincing the authorities a stray shot from a poacher's gun had been the cause. But who would suspect Jessica's death at the hands of a highwayman? Get rid of her before she bears Acton an heir, he thought for the hundredth time. Then Acton would be next. Yes, by God! Then Acton himself would die.

Meanwhile, back at Aynesworth, the principal object of McClean's hatred stared dumbfounded as Saunders announced, "Lord Orling, your Grace."

Orling came forward with a hearty greeting on his lips. "I hope I find you well, dear boy," he said cheerfully.

Slowly rising, Acton walked around his desk. "To what do I owe the pleasure of this call?" he asked coldly.

Lord Orling flushed. "I just dropped in to pay my respects," he said uneasily.

"State your business, Orling. My time is taken up, so be brief."

"Now, now, my boy. That's no way to greet your wife's relative. Are you not going to invite me to sit? Surely—"

"Please do," Acton said without a trace of emotion in his voice.

"That is better. Much better," Orling smiled, seating himself in Acton's chair beside the hearth. "Ah, the pleasures of a fire. As I often remarked to your wife's dear, departed mother, God rest her soul, there is nothing so cozy as warming one's feet on a chilly day."

"You did not come here to comment about the fire."

"No, indeed not, dear boy. I came from the urgings of my heart."

"You what!" Acton ejaculated, disbelieving.

"Indeed, it is so, I assure you. Since you so swiftly plucked my dearest Jessica from my bosom, I have found life lonely at Orling House."

"Good God!"

"It has proven a gloomy place, my boy. When I recall the sound of Jessica's dear voice singing about our home, I wonder how I can bear the loss."

"As I said, I am busy. We will terminate this interview."

"Now, see here, sir—"

"No! *You* see, Orling. I well know the pitiable manner in which Jessica lived while under your roof."

"No, no. She was my cherished—"

"When I realized how you'd treated her, I loathed you for the bounder you are. Were it not for Jessica, I would throttle you."

"You took my girl—" Orling came to an abrupt halt as the expression on Acton's face penetrated his consciousness. "Pray, my boy," he began weakly.

Leaning his shoulder against the wall, Acton negligently tapped one foot on the floor. "Your boy?" he asked softly.

"You—as my daughter's husband," Orling said shakily.

"Your daughter?" Acton purred.

"Stepdaughter, then. I always—I assure you, she was a daughter to me."

"You cur," Acton murmured, his tone level. "You have come for money."

"I—I fail to see why you should think—"

"I am not a fool."

"I would not sell—"

"You would. Your soul, if necessary."

"You owe me something," Orling chattered. "There was no marriage settlement—"

Turning sharply on his heel, Acton crossed to the bellpull. Orling's heavy breathing was the only sound in the room as they waited. "You rang, your Grace?" the butler asked, answering the ring.

"Lord Orling is leaving, Saunders. Conduct him to his carriage."

"I won't go," Lord Orling cried. "You'll pay me! I'll make you."

Opening the door, Acton motioned to a footman on duty in the hall. "Which will it be, Orling?" he calmly asked. "Will you walk, or shall we carry you out?"

"You haven't heard the last of this, Acton. I'll make you sorry. See if I don't."

"William," his Grace said, nodding toward Lord Orling.

"Keep your flunkey away from me," Orling cried, and ran out of the house.

"Well, I never!" William breathed.

"Your Grace, may I tender my apologies—"

"You may not, Saunders. You could not have anticipated such behaviour when you admitted Lord Orling."

"Thank you, your Grace."

Acton sighed as he resumed his seat behind the desk. Picking up a sheaf of papers, he swiveled the chair about until his back was to the room, and forced his mind to the pages he held in his hand.

Jessica, coming in search of him, paused in the doorway, enjoying the sight of his dark hair gleaming in the sunlight. Feeling eyes on him, he turned his head, then, smiling, immediately rose. "Did you wish to see me, my love?"

"Am I interrupting you?"

"I am never too busy for you, my dear."

"What was the reason for the shouting in the hall?"

"An unimportant matter," he replied, leading her to the sofa. Turning her to face him, he cradled her in his arms, and bent to her lips.

"Mercy," Emaline's voice spoke from the doorway. "And in the daytime, too."

Turning his head, Action raised his eyebrows, and languidly remarked, "You will forgive me, Emaline, if I tell you I find you a trifle *de trop*."

"Well, if you wish to know what I think—" Emaline began, advancing into the room.

"Do not let it distress you, my dear," he said politely, tightening his grasp around Jessica when she would have sat erect. "Stay where you are," he murmured in her ear.

"For heaven's sake, John," Emaline cried, "listen to me. I will not long disturb you, I promise you." Waving a clutch of papers before his face, she said dramatically, "Just read this!"

Glancing at the pages covered with slanting lines of closely scrawled handwriting, he sighed. "All of it, Emaline?"

"Oh, very well. I will relate its content. Mary Ellen is rather tedious at times, I will admit."

"I do not wish to appear uncooperative, but should I evince an interest in, er, Mary Ellen?"

"Do not be disdainful with me, John. Jessica, can not you talk to him?"

Struggling out of his arms, Jessica sat up, feeling slightly foolish. "Acton, you should pay Emaline the courtesy of your attention," she gently reproved.

"As you wish, my dear. Well, Emaline?"

"Mary Ellen—you do not know her, I apprehend—has written they will soon arrive. Jules Ames, and Andrew Lindsey, and, oh, several others."

"Let me see that!" Acton demanded, staring down at the papers Emaline thrust into his hand. "Good Lord!" he cried.

"Mary Ellen writes she intends accompanying them this far, and then will proceed on to visit me," Emaline explained. "A groom has just brought her letter which arrived at Marrivane Hall."

"Apparently they plan to surprise us. Does the letter say when they will arrive?"

"No, but it should be any day now, I'd say. If you ask me," Emaline continued vehemently, "they should allow you to remain private. I haven't the smallest doubt they will become a nuisance."

"You haven't?" Acton asked softly.

"Your meaning is perfectly clear," she smiled, moving to the door. "Pray continue."

"Do close the door behind you, Emaline," Acton chuckled. Gathering Jessica back into his arms, he said in a musing voice, "Now what was I about when we were interrupted?"

"You were behaving in a most peculiar fashion for an old married man."

"I will never become too old," he grinned.

"May I hold you to that?"

"Do you doubt it?" he murmured against her lips.

CHAPTER XVIII

Lord Orling sat sprawled on the seat, his wig askew, his eyes narrowed to slits, as he turned his head and stared unseeing through the window. The coach was traveling fast, whipped up by the coachman at his lordship's orders. Orling's head slumped forward, his chin sinking into the folds of a rumpled cravat. His lips tightened as his hands clenched a long ebony cane. Lost in bitter thoughts of Acton, nursing his hatred, he hardly heard the shot that made the horses whinny and lurch the coach to a stop. The door was jerked open, and the muzzle of a pistol thrust in and leveled at his lordship. "Don't try nothin' me 'earty," a rough voice snarled.

Orling turned his head and saw the grizzled face staring in at him. "What the devil do you want?" he growled.

" 'Ere now, what kind o' talk is that?"

Orling held a lace-edged handkerchief to his nose. "You smell, you—you goat!"

"Goat, is it? Now, see 'ere—"

"You will remove your presence from my sight. This instant, do you hear?" Orling raved, his voice rising.

"Ye're a rare gager, ye are. This be a—"

"Get away!" Orling screamed, beside himself with rage. Swinging the cane, he scarcely seemed to notice the roar of the pistol as a ball buried itself in the back of the seat beside his head. Climbing down from the coach, he advanced upon the highwayman, screeching profanities and pummeling his quarry about the head and shoulders.

"'Ere, now, wait up," the man begged backing away.

His lordship's coachman came running up, brandishing a pistol. "Put up your hands. Hold, I say," he ordered the would-be robber.

"Get this 'ere maniac off o' me," his victim implored.

"Your lordship—" the coachman began.

"Of course," said Lord Orling, collecting himself. "Come over here, you. I will have a word with you. You, Welks. Put that pistol away, and wait beside the coach."

Leading the robber to a copse beside the road, Orling sat down on a fallen log, and ran his eyes over the man. "You are not a pretty specimen, but I think you'll do. I am hiring you to perform a service."

"Now, see 'ere—"

"Or I could hand you over to the nearest constable."

"What's the lay?" the man hastily asked.

"I thought so. I presume you would feel no remorse for taking a life? No, of course you wouldn't, and I am willing to pay handsomely, I assure you. You have heard of his Grace, the Duke of Acton?"

"Ye mean ye want the Dook snabbered?"

"I want him dead. Also his Duchess."

"Gawd!" the highwayman breathed.

"If you find it beyond your powers to eliminate both of them, I will accept either one or the other. I do not care how or when."

"Lord luv us, yer honour. The Dook?"

"If you fail, I will see you hang from the highest scaffold. And not one guinea will you receive until you succeed."

"Where'll I find ye when I've done it?"

"I am Lord Orling. You will find me in London. I need not remind you of your fate, should you fail— or reveal my identity."

"Yer what?"

"My name, you fool."

Upon his newly acquired hireling's riding off in the direction of Aynesworth, he reentered his coach, his thin lips smiling slightly, and waved the coachman onward.

The following morning, Jessica sat perched up on Lottie, riding slowly beside Emaline through the sunlight, and followed at a discreet distance by Jenks and a younger groom named Jem. Jessica was pondering the problems posed by the coming influx of guests, while Emaline was wondering if the wardrobe she had brought with her would be sufficient to increased demands placed upon it. Turning the horses down a path through the wood, they were forced by the narrowness of the trail to ride in single file.

Admiring Jessica's habit as she followed along behind, Emaline remarked, "You really must give me the address of your dressmaker, dearest."

"When you are next in London, we shall visit Madame Francel," Jessica promised. "I think you will find her work to your liking."

"I am sure I shall. Austin will find my wardrobe in need of replenishment, I promise you. Babies are such darlings, but they do make inroads on one's supply of clothing."

"I am sure your figure has not suffered," Jessica smiled.

"Well, no, but—" Emaline's speech gasped to a halt as the sound of a pistol shot split the silence of the wood. The startled horses whinnied and shied at the sudden loud noise, giving their riders a moment of difficulty in controlling them until Jenks and Jem came pounding forward to grasp the bridles.

"That was a shot!" Jessica gasped, looking around fearfully.

"Do you think so?" Emaline quavered.

"Probably a poacher, my lady," Jenks answered with more assurance than he felt. "Let Jem accompany you home, your Grace, while I look around. The poacher will greatly regret his carelessness when I come across him."

"If you feel we should, Jenks—"

"Jem will take good care of you, your Grace," he assured her as he watched them mount up and ride off in the direction of Aynesworth. Dismounting, he moved slowly in the direction from which he judged the shot had been fired, and searched until he found the place where the culprit had lain in wait. Returning to his horse, he mounted and turned about to gallop fast on the return to Aynesworth.

Entering the hall, he nervously turned his cap in his hands, arguing in a low voice with Saunders, until the butler reluctantly conducted him to his Grace's study. Pausing before the door, Saunders fixed him with a stern eye. "It is not my custom to disturb his

his lordship unnecessarily, Jenks. You are quite certain—"

"What I have to tell his Grace is important," Jenks insisted.

"It had better be," Saunders told him severely, and rapped on the door. "Jenks requests an audience on a matter of importance, your Grace," he solemnly announced.

Acton looked up in surprise. "Can it not wait?" he inquired, indicating the estate manager seated in a chair across from his desk.

"I think you will wish to hear what I have to say immediately, your Grace," Jenks said as firmly as he could.

Acton studied him keenly. "Very well," he said. "If you will wait in the hall, Mr. Stallings. And if you will be so good as to close the door behind you."

When they were alone, Acton indicated the chair just vacated by the manager. "Now, what is this matter that could not wait?"

"Jem and I were accompanying her Grace and her ladyship on their ride," Jenks began, nervously twitching his cap in his hands as he perched on the edge of the seat.

Acton was suddenly very still. "Yes?" he softly prompted.

"We were riding through the wood, single file, your Grace, when a—pistol—was fired."

"The ladies?" Acton gasped.

"They are safe, your Grace. No one was injured."

Acton suddenly sat down hard in his chair, his knees feeling weak. "Go on," he murmured.

"I assured their ladyships it was a stray shot from a careless poacher, but I thought differently, your

Grace. So I sent their ladyships home with Jem, and looked around."

"And?"

"I found where someone had waited in ambush. The marks were clear, your Grace. The prints of a horse and of a man were there in the ground."

Acton sat staring into space as the silence lengthened. Finally he turned his gaze on Jenks. "A pistol, you say?"

"Yes, your Grace."

"Tell Saunders I wish Mr. Browning to wait on me immediately."

"Yes, your Grace," Jenks repeated, and hurried from the room, relieved to have the interview come to an end.

By the time the secretary entered the study, Acton had finished writing and folding a note, and was pressing the ducal seal into warm wax. "Come in, Aswold. I find myself in need of your opinion," he said, laying the note aside.

Acton's secretary waited, wondering at the grimness of his Grace's face. "Sit down, Aswold," Acton invited, then added with some humour. "You have not been summoned before the headmaster, you know."

Mr. Browning permitted himself a slight smile as he seated himself, then started to his feet as his Grace added, "Jenks has just told me of an attempt on her Grace's life. A pistol was fired at her this morning while she was riding with my sister. Fortunately, no one was injured."

"But who—"

"Ah, yes, Aswold. Not a poacher, I'm certain. Jenks found the spot where a man had waited in ambush. And he is certain a pistol was fired."

"A poacher would use a snare or trap."

"Exactly. Who comes to mind, Aswold?" Acton asked softly.

"Lord McClean," Mr. Browning answered without pause.

"We are of the same opinion, it seems."

"May I ask what her Grace has reported?"

"Nothing, as yet," Acton replied, then chuckled at his secretary's expression. "You will be relieved to know I expect her momentarily. Unless I am much mistaken, she is now debating the necessity of informing me. We will reassure her by encouraging Jenks' 'theory' of the poacher."

"What will you do concerning Lord McClean, your Grace?"

"I have prepared a note inviting him to wait upon me at his earliest convenience."

"He will arrive with all possible dispatch, I should think."

"Quite. His conceit is monumental. It would never occur to him that his presence is less than desirable." Acton paused for a moment, as if deciding how much of his plans he could reveal. "I plan to offer McClean an allowance. A very generous allowance, I might add."

"With the stipulation—" Mr. Browning smiled, leaving the thought unfinished.

"Precisely. Shall we say France, do you think, Aswold? On the other hand," Acton mused, "I count many Frenchmen among my friends. Perhaps we will permit McClean to select the arena of his exile. For the amount I am prepared to pay to insure her Grace's safety will reach beyond even his powers of refusal."

"You desire me to leave at once, your Grace?"

"No, Aswold. I think not. Allow me my small pleasures. A flunkey will deliver the note."

* * *

Acton's estimation of McClean proved most accurate. When he had read the missile, his expression underwent a noticeable change. Sending for his man Courtney, he issued orders in rapid succession and, within the brief span of three days, issued forth to survey his entourage drawn up before the door.

His gaze moved from the outriders garbed in the livery of the Alastair's to the ducal crest boldly emblazened upon the door of his coach. I have more right than Acton, he thought, as a satisfied look crept into his eyes. His gaze roamed to the coach following, piled high with the trunks and boxes containing his wardrobe; for McClean was sure his stay at Aynesworth would be a long one.

As he settled himself comfortably in his seat, a highwayman stood his hidden watch, concealed in a woods just beyond the outer boundary of Aynesworth; on perceiving the approaching entourage, he believed it to be that of his Grace. He mounted his gelding and drew a mask across his grizzled face, then pulled a pistol from his belt. Leaning forward in the saddle, he waited until the coach with the crest upon its door drew abreast, then drove his heels into his horse, sending it surging forward. Thundering down the slope, he rode straight for the coach, the pistol levelled. He leaned sideways from the saddle, and jerked open the door, firing straight into the face of the lone occupant, then wheeled and galloped away before McClean's lifeless body had time to fall to the floor.

The postilions dragged their frightened horses to a halt, but only that they might gaze after the departing horseman. None of them so much as fired a shot in return. The coachman struggled to bring his horses to a standstill, climbed down to the road, and gaped inside. Climbing back to the box, he whipped up the horses and continued on to Aynesworth.

"What happened?" the young groom asked.

"You don't need to know."

"Is he dead?" the groom insisted.

"Yes. Now be quiet."

CHAPTER XIX

One day, a week later, Jessica sat in the rose salon, a book lying forgotten on her lap. From the moment McClean's coach had arrived before the house with his lifeless body sprawled inside, life at Aynesworth had been more than a little strained. Convention had been satisfied by McClean's burial in the family mausoleum following private services attended by members of the family and the household staff, the Dowager Duchess supporting her sister-in-law not only on the journey from London but through the ordeal of the funeral as well. Following the services, however, Lady Eurice refused to leave her room for two days, after which she emerged to accuse Acton of seeking her grandson's death.

Jessica could only wonder at the tenacity with which Lady Eurice clung to her delusions in remembering her descendant as a kind and loving person. She would believe what she wished to believe, Jessica thought, sighing.

Acton's voice interrupted her thoughts. "Here you

are, my dear." Bending over to kiss her cheek, he chuckled. "Are you sitting and thinking, or just sitting?"

"I never just sit."

Acton cocked an amused eye at her. "Guarding your secrets, are you?" he said, seating himself beside her.

"No, dear. I was thinking of Lady Eurice."

"Then your time would be better spent just sitting. My disreputable relatives have proven more than a little hateful. I cannot find it in my heart to regret Mc-Clean. In fact, my dear, for his attempt against your life, I will never forgive him."

"Acton, about McClean. Do you suppose you were to be his—next victim?"

"McClean would never have exposed himself, had that been the case. You need have no fear on that score, Jessica. A highwayman saw the crest upon the coach and thought to acquire valuables, that is all."

"But he took nothing."

"We will never know why he fired, but one thing we do know. McClean's conceit proved his downfall."

Jessica felt as though she were throbbing all over with the relief Acton's words brought. The day seemed brighter and she was determined not to let unpleasant memories intrude on their happiness. "We have yet to have a honeymoon," Acton said, drawing her close against his side. "We will go abroad. How many days will you require to pack?"

"Two. Three at the most."

She barely had time to catch her breath before his lips fastened on hers in a kiss that deepened as desire rose up in him. He raised his head, and his eyes glinted into hers. "Come," he said.

"Where are we going?"

"Upstairs."

"Upstairs? But, why—"

"Don't argue, sweet," he said, and urged her somewhat rapidly up the steps. Entering her room, he nodded to Agnes. "Your services are not required at the moment."

Jessica looked at him in surprise while Agnes curtsied and hurried from the room. "Acton, what on earth—"

"Come here," he said with mock severity.

Approaching him cautiously, she glanced around, but could see nothing in the room to perturb him. "Is something amiss?" she asked.

"Very much so," he replied, a look of amusement upon his face. Pulling her against his hard frame, he placed both hands at her waist and held her to him.

"You are crushing my gown," she protested weakly.

"I'll buy you another," he murmured huskily, and swept her up into his arms.

Some time later he lay beside her, idly toying with a curl falling over one of her ears. Wrapping it around a finger, he slowly stroked it with his thumb. When she turned her head to gaze into his eyes, he said softly, "You will enjoy your honeymoon."

"Oh?" She smiled provocatively. "In what way, my Lord?"

"I shan't tell you," he replied, his eyes gleaming through half-opened lids. "Ladies must accept their punishment if they would lure the male."

"I know what's the matter with you," she said. "You're blind."

Acton's lips parted slightly. "Certainly not. Bedazzled by a seductive lady, perhaps."

Jessica cocked an eyebrow. "Only bedazzled, your Grace?" she whispered.

"No," he murmured, kissing her fingers one at a time. "Imprisoned for life by these small hands."

"If you are to escape, I should start packing."

He burst out laughing. "You adorable rogue," he said. "I do believe you will always have the last word."

"I no doubt shall," she concurred, jumping from the bed. "Up, sir, I beg you."

"But I am unreformably lazy, my dear."

"If you think I intend to dress you, you quite mistake the matter," she said, pertly cocking her head.

"Very well, my dear," he chuckled, rising from the bed. "It does seem a shame, though. I much prefer you without your clothes."

She giggled softly. "Do be quiet," she said. "We should tell Grandmama of our plans."

They found the Dowager Duchess in the blue salon. "So there you are," she said, laying aside her book. "I've been meaning to talk to you. It is my intention to return home, Alastair. At my age I long for the comfort of my own bed."

"You will do as you like, of course. Jessica and I came to inform you we have decided on a honeymoon. Will you drink a toast with us?" he asked, crossing to a table to pick up the decanter that stood on it.

"I have not become so ancient I cannot have a glass of wine when I choose. So you have decided to travel, have you. I well remember my own trips to the Continent. Your Grandpapa and I were quite gay in our youth, Alastair."

Jessica's eyes danced. "Quit the hoyden, were you?"

"A high-stepper of the first water, my dear."

"And still capable of bending hearts," Acton laughed. He turned his head as Saunders entered the room.

"Beg pardon, your Grace, but a party has this moment arrived at the door."

Acton groaned. "Is Lord Ames one of the group?"

"He is, your Grace. The party numbers some ten persons. I have shown them into the green salon."

"Order tea, Saunders. And wine for the gentlemen. We will come in a moment." Acton stared at Jessica, and waited until Saunders had bowed himself out before he said, "Shall I send them away?"

"You could scarcely do so without appearing rude," she replied with some regret, and went off on his arm to greet the guests.

Lord Ames immediately came over to them. "Your obedient servant, ma'am," he said. "Has Acton been treating you well? For if he hasn't, I'm thought to be quite eligible, you know," he added, grinning.

"Now, Jules," Acton chuckled, taking Jessica's hand in his. "You gave her to me, remember."

"Worst mistake of my life, I assure you. Tell you what, dear boy. Retire from the field while we're here, and I promise not to wear out my welcome."

"How long will you be with us?" Acton asked quietly.

Jules's eyes sobered as he gazed at him. "What's up, John?" he asked thoughtfully.

"McClean is dead. He was shot by a highwayman."

"Nonsense," Jules exclaimed, a great deal struck. "Why would a highwayman shoot McClean?"

"I rather imagine it was the ducal crest affixed to the door of his coach."

"You can't mean it!"

"I do. Anticipatory conceit, no doubt."

"So a ruffian thought to stop a duke, and bagged McClean. You know, Acton, there was always something mighty queer about your cousin."

Jessica, having noticed a footman rolling the tea cart in, moved across to pour. Their honeymoon must necessarily be postponed, she ruefully mused, though the presence of guests should ease the gloom that had settled over the house. Cheered by this thought, she glanced up to smile at Austin. "Quite a siege, isn't it?" he remarked after offering to carry around the plates. "Grandmama wants to know who all these people are."

"Tell her I have no idea," she replied, sighing to see Lady Eurice entering the room.

"I confess I do not understand this intrusion on our privacy," Lady Eurice said the moment she arrived by Jessica's side. "How you can think of food with dearest McClean—" Choking, she held a handkerchief to her swimming eyes.

"Let me ring for a maid," Jessica offered. "She will see you to your room—"

"Do not think to shuttle me off," Eurice answered irritably, while rapidly recovering from the vapors. "When I think of the loyalty I have given the family! And now, to be so cruelly thrust aside—" Eurice paused dramatically.

Thinking her performance worthy of the stage, Jessica wondered what was next to come. She was not long left in doubt.

"Clementine informs me I am being cast forth from Aynesworth," Eurice announced in aggrieved tones.

"I'm certain Grandmama would not—"

"Oh, she couched it in her usual platitudes, but her meaning was quite clear. Acton is seeking to evade his responsibilities." She paused, glancing around to assure herself that she had attracted the attention of nearby guests, then continued. "We all know his line descended from an illegitimate usurper. It could not be proven, but everyone knows—"

"Eurice," Grandmama said, taking her firmly by the arm. "You are not well. I will support you to your room."

"Let go of me! I am not so easily hoodwinked, let me tell you." Eurice glared venomously at Grandmama, then whirled on Acton. "Clementine should have given her jewelry to me. You had McClean killed before she could change her mind. Don't think I'm not on to your little schemes!"

"That will do." Acton's voice was calm. "Your grief has overset you, Aunt Eurice. We will talk later."

"I will talk, you may be sure. But with the law!"

"Come," Grandmama insisted, and hustled her from the room.

"Oh, I say, John," Lord Ames spoke into the silence that followed. "Your Aunt reminds me of my mother's cousin, a shocking loose screw. I can't think how she bumbled into the family."

"Every family has one, I'd say," Austin said. "With us, it was Papa's sister. When she married an Australian and left the country, it was the best thing that ever happened."

"Oh, I say, that's a capital idea," Lord Ames grinned at Acton. "About your Aunt, dear boy. Send her to Australia."

"If only I could," Acton replied, smiling slightly at the thought. "But since I can't, I will ask you to be so good as to come with me into my study. I have an idea I want to try out on you both."

They all three went across the hall, and into the room, Acton firmly closing the door behind them. Lord Ames and Austin immediately took a seat, but Acton stood at the window a moment, his hands loosely clasped behind his back, before he turned and went to his desk. He sat for a time immobile. At last, sighing very faintly, he said with an obvious effort, "I beg your pardon for seeming so glum. We Alastairs —God help us—must all appear to be mad."

"Now, my boy, we'll have none of that," Austin said emphatically. "No one ever bore you any ill will because of McClean."

"You need not frown at me, Austin. Were it not for Jessica, I shouldn't care. But with the threat hanging over our heads, I must get to the bottom of this mess. I believe I shall go mad myself if I do not."

"If you will but be patient, the authorities—"

"No," said Acton, with a rueful shake of his head. "The devil's in it now, make no mistake about that. My dear Aunt means mischief. She will see me damned if she can."

"Lady Eurice means to, right enough," agreed Lord Ames. "It's a puzzle to me, though, how she could accomplish it."

"I don't intend to wait around to find out, Jules. There is no saying what folderol she will take into her head to tell the authorities. Well, forget that. I want your opinion on an idea I have taken into my own head."

"Now this becomes interesting," remarked Lord Ames. "Could we be thinking the same thing, I wonder?"

"We could, if you are wondering whether McClean was mistaken for me and, in my place—I believe the term is snuffled? I have become convinced that it is only because he was that I am alive now."

"McClean must have played his cards badly," Austin said. "I always knew, of course, that he was a fool, but I never guessed how big a fool until now. He no doubt displayed a marked absence of common sense in selecting his murderer. But then, dog eat dog, eh?"

"Undoubtedly, Austin, but pray do not wax eloquent over it," Acton remarked, leaning back in his chair.

"But where's the good in not finding the outcome amusing, dear boy? Hoisted by his own petard, by God!"

"He does seem to have rather bungled the affair," Acton admitted reflectively. "I wonder what other plots he had in mind."

"John, McClean was a plaguey nuisance, but I shouldn't think it difficult to unravel his little schemes."

"And that, my dear Austin, brings us back to our original discussion. I find that I am desirous of paying a call at my departed cousin's home. It might be illuminating to discover what light McClean's servants can shed on the matter."

"Would not the Inspector already have questioned them?"

"The Inspector, as you may realize, Jules, is in no position to dangle coin of the realm under any man's nose. I, on the other hand, am under no such restriction. I plan to scatter money about most extravagantly until I get the answers I want."

"Then let's be about it," Lord Ames said eagerly, jumping to his feet. "I trust you mean us to accompany you?"

"Your impetuosity does you credit, Jules, but bear with me, pray. Tomorrow will suit us nicely. For the moment," he said, rising to walk with them out of the room, "we will honour the drawing room with our presence."

CHAPTER XX

Crowder was the name of McClean's coachman. Large of person and florid of countenance, he had never, in the memory of the household, bowed his head before any man. A very independent person was Mr. Crowder, and it was his boast that he had never, even at the risk of his position, taken the horses out, were not the weather fit. Altogether he was a quite celebrated coachman, perhaps the most celebrated one for miles around, and no one knew this better than Mr. Crowder.

Thus it was that, when summoned into the presence of the Duke, he came before him with head held high. Offended at the outset by his Grace's questions, from their insinuation that he might perhaps know something of his late lordship's movements, he turned first taciturn, and then almost completely uncommunicative. Upon his Grace's openly inquiring if he might have information not previously revealed to the authorities concerning the late lord's death, he became very thoroughly incensed. "Indeed, your Grace," he said as severely as he dared. "I cannot find it in my heart to speak ill of the dead, regardless how I might have felt about his lordship."

Acton became suddenly more at ease. "Now we are getting somewhere," he remarked, and fished his snuffbox from a pocket. Glancing keenly at Crowder, he flicked it open and held it forward. "Do you wish to try my snuff?" he invited pleasantly.

Crowder turned beet red. "Well, now," he stammered, much pleased, and more than a little surprised. "Your Grace—?"

"I insist," Acton answered with a sure understanding of the coachman's character. "I consider it a very good mixture. Perhaps you will concur."

Crowder nervously dipped a finger and thumb into the box. Spilling much of it on his sleeve, he nevertheless managed to convey enough for one nostril. "It is f-fine, your Grace," he said, and sneezed. "I am no judge in such matters, but—"

Acton, whose eyes had been fixed watchfully upon his face, smiled. "Nonsense," he said easily. "I'm quite prepared to take your word for it. I will send you a jar immediately upon my return home."

The air of aloofness fell from Mr. Crowder. Certainly, he told himself, he had all along intended to assist his Grace by imparting any information he might personally have to give. "Perhaps your Grace had not known about the crest upon his lordship's coach?" he hazarded to say.

"No, I rather fancy I hadn't."

Emboldened by the friendly expression on his Grace's face, Crowder continued confidingly: "I must say I could not approve, your lordship, and so I told

Mrs. Crowder, not once, but a hundred times, during this past year."

Acton became very still. He did not speak immediately, but when he did at last, it was with considerable restraint. "This past year?" he said briefly.

"Aye, your Grace. I felt it very forward of his late lordship, but seeing as how he seldom ordered the coach brought around, it didn't seem my concern."

"Then he did request that particular coach for his ill-fated journey to Aynesworth?"

"Of a certainty, your Grace. And mighty pleased he was, I'm sure." Crowder could not but be aware of the gravity of the Duke's face. He was looking stern, but there was something in his eyes which invited confidences. "I hope I'm not being hurtful of an innocent man, your Grace, but—if I may be so bold—I would question his late lordship's valet."

"May I ask why?"

"Courtney never seemed aboveboard, if your Grace takes my meaning. Oh, he pretended, right enough, but I know a rogue when I see one."

"Have you discussed this with the authorities?"

"No, your Grace. But," Crowder hastened to add when he saw the Duke's face harden, "I didn't know about the ruffian Courtney brought into the house shortly before his late lordship's death. The butler could tell your lordship about that. Mr. Meeks would have been the one what opened the door."

"I will have a talk with him, thank you, Crowder. But first I will have a word with Courtney."

"Well, now, your Grace, Courtney isn't here. He took off as soon as he learned his lordship was dead. I expect you'll find him at his sister's, over to Agecroft way."

Acton stood still as a statue, a dawning gleam coming into his eyes. Slowly a sardonic smile curled his lips. "I see," he said with only the slightest inflection. "Would you be so good as to tell me whether you have driven Lord McClean to the same vicinity?"

"Aye, your Grace, I have. His lordship accompanied Courtney to his sister's place on several occasions."

"I am going to ask you another question, Crowder, and I want you to think very carefully before you reply. The answer could be important." Acton paused, his gaze locked with the coachman's. "Have you ever driven Lord McClean to the Hare and Hounds?" he finally said softly.

Crowder scratched his head, deep in thought. "Aye, your Grace. Once, that I can remember."

"Now think carefully, man. Which coach did his lordship order that one time?"

" 'Twas the one with your Grace's crest upon the door. I remember particularly because it was at night. His lordship only used that coach at night."

"You will swear to that?"

"But of course, your Grace. I didn't see any harm—"

"Harm!" Acton took a deep breath, steadying himself. "I crave your indulgence for one further question, Crowder. I will ask you if anything untoward took place at the Hare and Hounds that evening."

"Now you mention it, your Grace, it did. I heard tell murder was done that night. Terrible it must of been, from what I hear."

Acton walked across the room and held out his hand. "You have rendered me a valuable service, Crowder. Shall we shake hands on it?"

Crowder slowly put out his hand, very red of face. "I'm sure I'm glad if I have, your Grace. I didn't suspicion—is it possible his late lordship—?"

"Extremely possible, Crowder," Acton replied honestly. "But since you have yet to give testimony to the authorities, I wish that you will not mention it to anyone. It could do no good, and might result in Courtney's being alerted. We wouldn't want him to skip the country before he can be questioned, eh?"

"No, sir, your Grace. We wouldn't, for a fact. I won't even tell my Missus."

"Thank you, Crowder. That will no doubt be best," Acton said as the coachman bowed himself from the room.

Deep in thought, he swung around on his heel and began to pace about, his long strides speaking clearly of the agitation of his mind. Lord Ames stretched out his long legs and leaned back in his chair, watching Acton's perambulations from beneath lowered lids. Lord Marrivane, flicking open his snuffbox, took a pinch. "Do sit down," he said cheerfully, "before you wear a path in the carpet."

Acton came to a halt beside a chair. "As I see it," he said, sitting down, "we have nothing to gain by questioning the servants further. The butler—what was his name?"

"Meeks," supplied Lord Ames.

"Yes. Well. It can be argued that this Meeks may be hand in glove with Courtney. He must have known there was something smokey in a ruffian having discourse with McClean, yet he said nothing of it to the Inspector. Does that not strike you as odd?"

"Exceedingly odd," said Austin. "And since it does, we will not wish him aware of the knowledge we have gained."

"Exactly. The Inspector may have a considerable interest in questioning him further." Acton studied Lord Ames briefly. "I think, Jules," he said, smiling slightly, "that you are about to say—I am nearly sure you are about to say—that you would like nothing better than to post to London to call upon the Inspector."

"I am not in the least interested in posting to London, dear boy. However, were I to go in your curricle, and behind your greys—"

"My greys?" murmured Acton.

"Oh, very well," grinned Jules. "Your bays."

The interview with Crowder swept away the despair that had been hanging over Acton for weeks. The day was fine, the future loomed bright, and he would shortly see Jessica's face when he told her the news. There was a suggestion of a strut in his walk when he sallied forth and swung up into the saddle. By the time they reached Aynesworth, he had formulated in his mind exactly what he would say to Jessica, and what she would say in reply.

What she said, the moment she saw him, was, "How nice you look, Acton. Is your neckcloth tied in a special way?"

Driven into the corner, he nevertheless fought back. "Do you know, Jessica Alastair," he said, wading in bravely. "You are tempting providence."

Jessica, far from worsted, looked at him inquiringly. "I am?" she said innocently.

This gave him the opening for which he'd been waiting. "I have a very good notion not to tell you my news," he said, throwing his best Sunday punch.

The blow fell wide of the mark. Jessica eyed him in triumph. "Then I shan't press you," she said smugly. "Wives should never meddle in what doesn't concern them, won't you agree? I once heard of a case—"

"Come here, you deplorable little scapegrace, and

let me put your mind at rest," he said, with a glow in his eyes that warmed her heart.

"Silly," she said, putting her hand in his. "Did it never occur to you that my mind has ever been at rest?"

"Your faith, my love—God! What it has meant to me! You cannot know—"

"I do hope you aren't getting ready to tell me," she told him frankly. "How very tiresome that would be. Well, come and sit down, Acton, and tell me what you learned at McClean's."

"Vixen!" he said. "Do you know everything I do?"

"For the most part, yes," she replied composedly. "Perhaps that is not quite accurate," she added thoughtfully. "I rather fancy I know everything you do. Do you think I wouldn't? You rode over this morning with Jules and Austin—"

"Don't gloat," he murmured, and cut off further utterances from her tongue by sealing her lips with his. Jessica thereupon did become most cooperative, and listened to his every word with concentration. They were sitting down by the time he concluded, her head resting against his shoulder and sheltered within the circle of his arms.

"I knew how it would be," she said contentedly, entwining her fingers with his. "I am married to an honourable man, it seems."

"That you are, my dear," he replied, sighing softly. "I had thought my name might never be cleared."

"It seemed to me highly nonsensical for you to have been so worried. I quite depended on the truth coming out."

"You must forgive me for putting you through a

horrid time. I trust any recollections your memory calls up are not too painful."

Turning in his arms, she regarded him with a twinkling eye. "There is something," she said in a teasing voice. "About an heir—"

CHAPTER XXI

Upon the occasion of Lord Ames's return to London, he was received by Saunders, who showed no emotion at sight of the gentleman whose errand to London had meant so much to his Grace. Saunders, in the way of all good butlers, would never demean himself by betraying the least interest. But in the course of time, by means known only to himself, he would always become as conversant with his Grace's affairs as was his Grace himself. He bowed to his lordship in a stately way, conducted him across the hall, and held open the library door. "Lord Ames, your Grace," he announced in noncommittal tones.

Acton was seated at his desk in the act of affixing his signature to a document placed before him by Mr. Browning. He looked up, read the tired but happy expression on Lord Ames's face, and smiled. "Have a seat, Jules. I will be with you in a moment," he said, indicating the as yet unsigned papers in the secretary's hands. "Help yourself to the Madeira."

Lord Ames poured himself a glass, took a chair be-

side the fire, and leaned back at ease, crossing one ele-
gantly clad leg over the other. As he sipped, an expression of supreme contentment crossed his face. His gaze
dreamily roamed the room, coming at last to rest upon
his friend. Acton, as he well knew, was not the easy-
going exquisite which many thought him. More than
one hapless opponent had discovered to his regret
that his air of lazy indifference concealed an astute-
ness of mind and strength of purpose quite at variance
with his seeming preoccupation with the more frivolous side of life. Jules watched his well-manicured
hand guiding the quill across the bottom of the final
sheet, and sighed.

"Papa would be pleased with you," he said.

Acton laid down the pen, and remarked, with the
glimmer of a smile, "Browning keeps me so damnably
busy. I am sure you perceive my problem."

"If that is meant to make me feel for you, dear boy,
I must tell you it doesn't. I daresay Browning deserves
my sympathy."

The secretary hastened to gather up the papers.
"Will your Grace wish my further service?" he asked
respectfully.

"Not at all," Acton said, getting up from his chair
behind the desk. "You have already worked me much
too hard for one day."

Mr. Browning bowed and went out, while Acton
strolled across the room to join Lord Ames. "I am inclined to hazard the opinion that you have good news
for me."

"The best," Lord Ames replied, grinning. "I left
the Inspector on the point of displaying a deplorable
lack of self-restraint. He seemed to think you a para-
gon of sleuths."

Acton reached a hand into his pocket for his snuffbox. "It occurs to me, Jules, that though the Inspector may be an addlepate, you did not come here to tell me of it."

"No," admitted Jules. "I came to tell you that Courtney has been apprehended."

Acton took a pinch of snuff, and carefully dusted his fingers. "You will no doubt give me the details in your own good time," he remarked suavely.

"As usual, you are right. I won't keep you in suspense. Courtney has confirmed McClean's presence at the Hare and Hounds the evening of the murders, though he had the foresight to insist he waited in the coach on McClean's orders."

"I should think he would."

"True," agreed Lord Ames. "I shall own myself surprised if Crowder substantiates his claim."

"What did the Inspector have to say about McClean's murder?"

"I told him you believed it was a case of mistaken identity. He found that extremely illuminating, and begs you will accept his felicitations. I think that Courtney and Meeks will find themselves unable to withstand him. The Inspector may be a slowtop in some ways, but once he scents his quarry, he can be damnably tenacious."

"Then we shall soon see an end to the affair. My dear Jules, I am obliged to you," Acton added earnestly.

"Nonsense," Lord Ames said promptly. "Pray do not insult me. There *is* one thing, if you would remain in favour."

Acton gave a hearty laugh. "I might have known," he said. "Well, what is it?"

"Not it. She. The entrancing blond I saw ascending the stairs when I crossed the hall."

"That would be Lady Carnaby, Emaline's friend."

"I trust her name is Phoebe. It should be, you know."

"Not at all. It is Mary Ellen."

"Good God! What could her mother have been thinking of? Phoebe is a better notion."

"I'm sorry you disapprove," Acton remarked affably. "Do you still wish to know her?"

"I shall call her Phoebe," Jules said in reflective tones. "But not at first, you understand. I shouldn't want to frighten her away before I succeed in winning her notice."

"No doubt your father will be pleased. I take it you have found your chit?"

"Obviously," said Jules.

"In that case, you will be advised to include your person in this afternoon's excursion. As I understand it, Andrew Lindsey has hastened to do so."

"If Andy fancies himself her suitor, he is doomed to disappointment."

"Naturally," said Acton, "he is doomed to disappointment."

Upstairs, Emaline was taking an unconscionable time dressing. If an impetus had been needed to strengthen her resolve, the presence of Mary Ellen was it. Considerably struck by her friend's graceful form and youthful bloom, Emaline had surveyed her own reflection with unprecedented severity, uttered one derogatory epithet under her breath, and plunged into her wardrobe, to emerge with her arms piled high with gowns of every conceivable style and colour. Disregarding the wide-eyed amazement of her maid, she spent a full half hour struggling into and out of half a dozen of them before deciding upon one. By the time she came downstairs, Jessica and Mary Ellen were seated in the carriage, Jules and Andy were vying with each other for Mary Ellen's attention, Acton and Austin were grimly waiting, and a groom was walking the gentlemen's mounts. The sight brought a frown between Emaline's brows.

Since the birth of her youngest (darling though she was), she had experienced a depression of spirits which was due, she knew, more to the prospect of encroaching age than to any impairment in her beauty. Her face, framed by artfully contrived curls peeping from beneath a high-crown bonnet, still retained its girlish look, and her figure, though not yet returned to its former profile, would, she felt sure, shortly do so. Suddenly realizing oneself a matronly mother of three could not be expected to lift the cloud. The years were tacking on, could not be blinked away. It was not that thoughts of Austin disturbed her very much. The admiration in his eyes was there for anyone to see as she ascended into the carriage in a blue spencer over her muslin gown. Emaline became aware the others were glancing at her questioningly, and smiled. She was too well-bred to allow a perturbed countenance to lessen the pleasure of the others in the excursion, and embarked on a discussion with Jessica of the shopping available in the village.

It was to be expected that neither Lord Ames nor Lord Lindsey would evince any disposition to abandon the field in the struggle for Mary Ellen's attentions. As luck would have it, Lord Lindsey, whose place beside Mary Ellen had been taken by Lord Ames in the confusion of introductions, was now astride the smaller horse. Short of the position being relinquished in his favour, there was little he could do to regain Lady Carnaby's ear other than to crane his head around Lord Ames and add what he could to the conversation. Under such circumstances the most optimistic suitor would have grown discouraged. By the time the village came into view, Lord Lindsey knew himself out of the running, and gave up the struggle.

McCauley was instructed to set the ladies down at the ribbon shop. By the time a selection had been made and an assortment of taffeta flowers purchased, it was time to stroll down the street in the direction of the tea room. It was naturally impossible to pass Miss Tweesdale's window without pausing to admire the bonnets on display. A lively discussion ensued concerning the proprietress' magic with a length of gauze, and the ladies went inside to try on very nearly every hat in the shop. Mary Ellen, entranced with a delectable concoction that framed her face in the most enchanting way imaginable, found herself quite unable to resist. The purchase made, there was nothing left to do but proceed to the tea room.

Thus it was that when they at last arrived, they found the gentlemen (with the exception of Jules) awaiting them with ill-concealed impatience. Jules's impatience was in no way connected with the fact that he had been left kicking his heels for the better part of half an hour, a strong desire again to behold Mary Ellen's face being at the root of it. The years of thinking himself proof against a female's charms had been wasted. He had been in love almost from the instant of clapping eyes on her. One glance at the arrested expression on his face poignantly affected her and made her feel shy as she approached their table.

Jules lifted her fingers to his lips, holding them in his warm clasp perhaps longer than good manners allowed. Mary Ellen firmly removed her hand. However eligible and handsome he might be, she was accustomed to flattering attention. "I had not the least notion of offering you an insult," he murmured audaciously.

Mary Ellen was covered with confusion. Until now the gentlemen of her acquaintance had limited themselves to heaping compliments upon her pretty head. She glanced at him in time to catch sight of a devilish twinkle in his eye. "Do you have something to say for every occasion, my lord?" she asked, taking the chair he pulled back for her.

"I shall have a great deal to say, but at a future time," he remarked, sitting down beside her.

She could find nothing to say in reply. Knowing that his lordship, an experienced man-about-town, turned a pretty phrase as readily as he breathed, she decided the most sensible course for her to follow, if she hoped to pique his interest, would be to accept his attentions with indifference. But realization that she did indeed wish to engage his notice caused her to flutter her lashes and lower her eyes. His lordship, needless to say, was enchanted.

Jessica, watching with surprise, caught Acton's eye and leaned toward him. "How perfectly odious you are," she said very low. "When did Jules first evince an interest in Mary Ellen?"

"The moment he saw her. It was a clear case of love at first sight."

"And to think I thought him a confirmed bachelor," she said, glancing at Emaline's friend. "I'll see to it that they are placed side by side at dinner."

"Don't worry your head over it," he replied. "Jules can manage his own affairs."

He did appear perfectly capable of doing so, Jessica was forced to admit. Though it was obvious his interest lay wholly with Mary Ellen, he made no move to give her his entire attention. He conversed affably throughout tea, alternating his remarks among the ladies, neither embarrassing Mary Ellen by paying her compliments before the others, nor throwing her into the dismals from neglect. He did walk beside her when they left the tea room and strolled down the street, making it plain he meant to hand her into the carriage himself. Mary Ellen's eyes shone.

Emaline, it seemed, had also noticed. "Lord Ames appears to have succumbed," she remarked to Mary Ellen when, with the gentlemen mounted alongside, the carriage had been turned around and was proceeding back along the street towards home.

Mary Ellen turned a happy face toward her. "Then you do not think he is only flirting with me?" she asked expectantly.

"You're forgetting, dearest, that a gentleman would never publicly exhibit a *tendre* for a lady unless he were serious. And I must say, I would like it above all things. With Jules and Acton such close friends, we would be bound to see a deal of you."

A happy sigh escaped Mary Ellen. Although she'd thought his lordship had looked at her in a special way, she had not been absolutely sure. She became more certain of it when, as the traffic lightened, the gentlemen pulled their mounts closer to the carriage, that they might converse, and she read the expression in his eyes.

Jessica, however short her acquaintance with Mary Ellen had been up to now, was not ill-pleased with developments. The wife of any friend of Acton's would necessarily be much in their company, and she did not doubt it would prove a pleasant relationship. She turned her gaze toward Acton, intending some remark —and stiffened, her eyes horrified as she stared at a spot somewhere beyond his shoulder. "Oh no!" she breathed, stunned. "It cannot be!"

The others, startled, followed the direction of her gaze, and, except for Acton, perceived nothing that should have caused such perturbation. "What on earth —" Emaline began.

"Do you see him, Acton?" Jessica whispered, looking rather pale.

"Yes," he said, lips tight. "Austin, the man entering the inn. Take careful note of his face."

"You mean the ruffian?" Austin asked in disbelief. "Why should I care to memorize his countenance?"

Acton cast him a warning glance. "We may need to describe him to the innkeeper," he explained for the benefit of the ladies. "For my part, I can't welcome his sort hanging about the village."

"Quite," agreed Austin, going along with the subterfuge. "We will tell Wilkins we disapprove of his being made welcome at the inn."

Jessica, recovering her poise, briefly commented on her own surprise at perceiving such a vulgar creature, and began at once to talk in her vivacious way on any number of subjects, continuing until Aynesworth was reached. Shortly after their arrival, it was time to go upstairs to dress for dinner, and so she had no opportunity to speak privately with Acton.

She did not join the whist party after dinner, but went instead into the drawing room to listen to others of their guests relating how they had spent their day. Her eyes wandered by chance to the end of the room where Mary Ellen was seated in conversation with Lord Ames, but of Acton she saw no sign. She was just on the point of going to look for him when Lord Lindsey came up to request she join him at cards.

She rose at once and went with him into the next room, and so had no opportunity of seeing Acton until, close on midnight, the party broke up and they all went up to bed.

"What is he doing here?" she demanded the instant he came into her room. "I recognized him as that horrid creature from the accommodation coach the moment I saw him."

"There is no need to worry," he remarked, crossing to seat himself in a chair beside her dressing table.

"Don't be absurd," she replied, stripping the bracelets from her wrist. "I do not want for sense, and to think to fob me off is a great piece of foolishness."

"I was not under the impression that I thought to," he said mildly. "If you want the truth, my dear, I was planning, given the opportunity, to acquaint you with developments."

"Then you are absolved," she said with a self-conscious little laugh. "It's just that I have been so anxious."

"Why shouldn't you be? I am. I have taken Austin into my confidence," he added gravely. "He will visit the village in the morning to search for the man. I do not deny I would prefer going myself, but the sight of my face could send him into hiding. Austin, on the other hand, is unknown to him."

Her hands stilled in unclasping the necklace. "What will Austin do when he locates him?" she asked after a slight pause.

"Jenks goes with him. They will bring the man here."

She removed the necklace. "Bringing such a creature into the house will cause talk," she said, rather surprised.

"My dear, it would be wonderful if I intended that. He will be taken to the stables, but that is beside the point. Austin may be forced to linger in the village for the better part of tomorrow. I feel it would be best if Emaline knows nothing of it."

"You would like me, I gather, to keep her occupied."

He turned a singularly gratified gaze upon her face. "It would be helpful if she were away from the house. Is there not someone you could visit, I wonder?"

"I know of no reason why we could not visit the tenants. As a matter of fact, Emaline has mentioned it."

He got up, and bent to press a kiss upon her nape. "Man's privileges should be held sacred," he remarked, crossing to the door leading to his dressing alcove.

"Oh?" she said archly. "Are your privileges being trampled on, sir?"

"Continually," he said succinctly, and left the room.

CHAPTER XXII

The hours dragged past without bringing any word from Austin. Acton closeted himself with Mr. Browning in the morning, and gave at least a part of his attention to the correspondence the secretary was attempting to cope with. Browning had not seen his Grace during recent days, and so had no notion of what could be distracting him. He did not appear to be in questionable health; his eyes had a tired look to them and he seemed a trifle pale, but the secretary put this down to the number of guests in the house. He experienced a strong feeling of sympathy, but forced himself to hide it. Nothing, he knew, would be more repugnant to his lordship. The correspondence disposed of, Browning drew a sheaf of bills from a portfolio. "Your Grace, if you will but glance over the accounts?" he ventured in hopeful tones.

"Why?" Acton said, a sudden smile hovering about his lips.

"I have not your authority to settle them," Browning replied, braving the amusement in his lordship's eyes.

"Do not despair, Aswold," Acton remarked, and smiled disarmingly. "I am sure you will find the means to pay them."

The secretary looked startled. "Of course, your Grace," he said, glancing away.

There came a moment's silence. "I was sure you would know of Lord Marrivane's errand," Acton observed, leaning back at ease in his chair. "Don't tell me it had escaped your notice."

Browning met the quizzical look in his lordship's eyes, and nodded. "I did know of it, your Grace," he admitted.

"Your discretion does you credit, Aswold. I need not have mentioned it."

At that moment the door opened to admit Austin. "I have good news, Acton," he said. Then he perceived the secretary. "I'm afraid I thought you alone," he added, coming to a halt.

"Browning is a prince among secretaries," Acton replied. "In any event, I'm sure he knows enough; you need not be secretive. What have you discovered?"

Austin looked flustered, but said, "The man did indeed put up at the inn. The proprietor assured me he appeared in the village several days ago, and has been hanging about ever since."

"Then our suspicions have been confirmed. Did you bring him back with you?"

"No, for he disappears during the day for hours at a time. I left Jenks to watch for him. In my opinion it will occasion less alarm among the ladies if you send McCauley to join Jenks. It may be nightfall before the man returns to the inn."

"See to it, Aswold," Acton said in a constrained voice. "McCauley is to use any means at his disposal to collar the fellow. When he is safely in custody, word will be sent to me from the stables."

The secretary met his look fully. "May I offer my services, sir?" he said, gathering up his papers.

"No, my dear boy, you may not. You will find ample opportunity to join in the fun later."

"Very well, your Grace," Browning replied, masking his disappointment as he went out of the room.

When they were alone Austin said in rallying tones, "Don't worry, Acton. Jessica is well guarded, so you may have a quiet mind."

"Good God!" Acton ejaculated, pressing his fingers to his temples. "Do you think I've had a moment's peace since we learned a ruffian was lurking about?"

"The thing is," Austin said soothingly, "we do know of him."

"I understand what you're saying, Austin. Lord! Jessica has been in danger every moment since I married her!"

"What can that signify? I don't imagine she would let it faze her."

"I know," Acton said in softened tones. "Had I known what lay before us, I would have married her regardless. I couldn't help myself, you see."

If he expected to find Jessica living in fear, he soon discovered his mistake. She was enjoying herself hugely. Never having been involved in intrigue before she thought nothing could equal the excitement of persuading a person to do one thing to keep her from finding out something else. She was very much inclined to think that, otherwise, Emaline would have made a wretched disclosure of their affairs. Having most properly guided her through treacherous shoals,

Jessica felt disposed to congratulate herself. There could be no doubt. She had the aptitude.

When she went down to dinner some two hours after her return to the house with Emaline, she was able to converse pleasantly with the guests, but it was a difficult thing to be obliged to do so when she wanted nothing better than to quiz Acton on the day's developments. By the time they sat down at table, she was all agog with curiosity. She could have wished the meal less protracted, but even it could not go on forever. It was with a great deal of anticipation that she went with the ladies to the drawing room, leaving the gentlemen to their port, and sat down to await their rejoining them.

Acton, as might be supposed, had no intention of enlightening her. He had two reasons for this: first, that any disclosures he might make could be overheard; and second, Jessica would insist upon seeing it through. He was conscious of a growing feeling of frustration as the evening wore on. The evening was no different from any other. The assembled company chatted, played cards, and consumed a copious amount of wine from the cellars. As he strolled among the guests his eyes went often to the door, but when finally Saunders approached to speak softly to him, his features remained unchanged.

Jessica, watching, intercepted the glance he threw at Austin, and arrived at the door before him. "Am I not coming with you?" she asked, looking at him with an accusing expression in her eyes.

"You may safely leave it to us, my dear," he replied, and went out through the door.

Jessica followed him into the hall. "I want to come along," she persisted. "After all—"

"I don't want you there," he interrupted to say flatly. "It will not be pretty."

"I don't care a snap for that," she said positively.

"No, Jessica," he answered quietly, leaving her no choice but to return to the drawing room.

Entering the stable office, Acton swept the ruffian with a cold gaze. He was not surprised by the man's appearance. Grizzled grey hair hung lankly above a wizened countenance made even less prepossessing by a long nose and sunken cheeks.

"You, I fancy, must be the stranger from the village," he remarked in silken tones. "I admit to being a trifle curious as to your purpose. You will relieve my apprehensions, I feel sure."

The man was staring at Acton with terror in his small, close-set eyes. "Just visitin'," he mumbled, while clutching his cap in nervous hands.

"*Your Grace*," Acton shot at him.

"Yer Grice," the man added grudgingly.

"That is better. Now perhaps you will expect to reckon with me. Your error in misjudging your adversary was really most foolhardy. I will see you hang for the attempt on her Grace's life. An inquiry into the murder of Lord McClean Alastair might also be advisable."

The ruffian's startled gaze, which had been flickering from face to face with swift glances, settled upon Acton. "I didn't snabble 'em, yer Grice," he objected in strident tones.

"I think there is a strong possibility that you did. However, we will pass over that for the moment. I will ask you what you were doing in the village. This time I expect an honest answer."

"I don't mind tellin' ye that, yer Grice, seein' as

'ow I didn't do no murder. I be seein' if there be a ken to slum."

"If you mean you were searching for a house to rob, do not suppose a jury would believe that," Acton said in matter-of-fact tones. "The entire village does not boast a cottage worth the effort. There are, in fact, only three houses in the entire district worthy of your talents. One belongs to the Squire, but I shouldn't advise your attempting it. Squire's temper has been made erratic by the gout, and he is a crack shot. Endeworth, some five miles distant, is, as I am sure you know, a veritable fortress. Even a craven such as yourself would hardly be so bold. That leaves Aynesworth. Surely you did not think to break in here?"

"I never seen a ken I'd liefer mill, yer Grice, what with its easy glazes and 'andy jiggers."

"I presume you are speaking of windows and doors. You may be somewhat hard pressed to come up with an answer, but that is spreading it a trifle thick. I'm sure you will agree. If you know what is good for you, my man, you will tell me the truth. Who hired you, and why?"

"I weren't 'ired by no one, yer Grice. I done told ye I weren't, d'ye see?"

"The memory no doubt eludes you," Acton remarked implacably. "I will refresh it. Lord Alastair— a most unreliable employer, I assure you—hired you to do away with—was it myself, or her Grace? It really does not matter; we will proceed to the identity of your victim. His lordship, a most foolish individual, set forth upon the road in a coach with, for reasons best known to himself, the ducal crest emblazoned upon its doors. An odd thing to do, you will agree.

I would imagine, correct me if I'm wrong, he had hired you to shoot us as we rode in our coach. A pity. He might well have succeeded in his purpose had he thought to inform you of his plans. You must have received a grievous shock on learning that you had slain the hand that fed you."

" 'Tweren't me, yer Grice. I be tellin' ye true," the man said, for the first time looking Acton straight in the eye. "I did 'ear tell o' the cove what done it. Mistook 'is man, 'e did, ye're right about that, yer Grice. I 'ear 'e left these parts. 'E won't be back, yer Grice. 'Twouldn't be safe."

Acton took a pinch of snuff. "I'm inclined to believe you," he said reflectively. "We will proceed on the assumption that you are innocent of involvement with Lord Alastair. That does not, however, close the book on you, if I may say so. 'If not in the pay of one, then in the pay of another,' would be your motto. I can only trust we will discover who the other is. To make certain of it, we will proceed in a different manner. Tell me who hired you, and I will rehire you. I have a shrewd suspicion your loyalty is for sale."

The assembled company gaped. A somewhat ghastly smile came upon the face of the ruffian. "Would yer Grice say—as much as what?"

"Double your pay from your previous employer. I need hardly add I will be buying our safety from you, in future."

"Well, now," the man said in a bewildered voice. "Ye'd not set the law on me?"

"Not unless you refuse my offer."

"Me price be twenty quid."

"You would kill for—well, never mind. I will pay you forty."

"Bloke says 'e be Lord Orling. Says 'e bides in Lunnon. 'E be a queer 'un, 'e be."

Acton seemed to sigh. He gazed at the man with a kind of dazed incredulity in his eyes. Recovering, he said to Austin, "Will you be so good as to ask Browning to bring the required sum? And now," he added to the ruffian, "I would like to know how you met Lord Orling."

"Well, yer Grice, I done stopped 'is rabbler, spectin' a fat truss, I were, seein' as 'ow 'e be a flash cove. I been a bridle cull since I be a young 'un, yer Grice, but never did I see a cove the likes o' 'im."

"If I follow you, you held up his coach expecting a fat purse. I take it you were disappointed."

" 'E come at me like ye'd not believe, yer Grice. Fair shocked, I were. 'E says 'e be wantin' ye dead, yer Grice. Yer Lidy, too."

"I have been blind indeed," Acton said in a grim voice. "It had not crossed my mind that we were doubly in jeopardy. We will pass over that then to Lord Orling's plot against us. I can well imagine what transpired. For reasons which I shall not divulge to you, his lordship committed the imprudence of contracting with you in an effort to settle his quarrel with me. I imagine he arranged for our deaths in exchange for not turning you over to the authorities. How he succeeded in overpowering you does not interest me in the least, though I would not be far from the mark in commenting on your singular ineptness at your trade. I believe your first attempt to dispose of her Grace was a shot from ambush. Your lack of skill with a pistol is obvious, but you would not have received an opportunity to correct your aim. What you were about in spying upon her Grace at the inn remains a puzzle, but I am not a fool. Her Grace has been care-

fully watched over ever since. Did you imagine you
would not be recognized in the village?"

" 'Is lordship did 'ire me, but I ain't sayin' I did
them other things."

"Possibly, but immediately you receive your pay,
and I see Browning has arrived with it, you will leave
these parts. I need not remind you of the consequences
should you again molest us."

"You can rest easy, yer Grice. You and yer Lidy be
safe from me," the man said, pocketing the money.
Crossing to the door, he added, "If ye wants me advice, yer Grice, I'd keep me winkers on that Lord
Orling, if I was you."

Some time later, Jessica was seated before the mirror
at her dressing table dreamily gazing at her image
when Acton came in through the door and sat down
in a chair by the fire. "I have something to say to
you," he said, and waited until she took a chair facing
him. "I regret the anxieties you have endured since
our marriage."

"I do not count them of importance," she answered,
puzzled.

"Yes, I know. Still, I would have had it otherwise."
He leaned back, his eyes half-closed, as he studied her.

"I do wish you would tell me what has happened,"
she said quietly.

His eyes were keenly alert, sensitive to the expression he read in her face. "You are entitled to the
truth. After Austin returned from the village, I sent
McCauley to join Jenks. They brought the man here
tonight, as you already know." Pausing, he searched
for the right words.

Jessica smoothed the fabric of her gown, quietly
waiting. Seeing his eyes on her hands, she folded them
carefully together and held them still.

"The man admitted he had been hired to do us harm," he continued finally.

"Us?" she exclaimed, staring at him, startled.

"I have doubled his pay and he is now in my employ. He has left the vicinity and will not trouble us again."

A terrible premonition seized Jessica. "Who hired him?" she whispered.

Silence hung heavy in the room before he said, "I am sorry, dearest. It was Orling."

Jessica, white, pressed her fingers to her cheeks. "It would be, of course. What will you do now?"

"I leave for London in the morning. I must work something out with Orling."

"You will not harm him? I wouldn't care one bit if you did, but I should not want you arrested."

"I will not call him out, I promise you. He is your stepfather, however unfortunate that may be. I will not create a scandal." Rising from his chair, he pulled her up into his arms. "I will return the day after tomorrow. I promised you a honeymoon, remember."

"What of our guests?"

"They must fend for themselves," he murmured against her lips. "Now, stop talking."

CHAPTER XXIII

The day appointed for Acton's return came and went with no sign of him. On the evening of the second day, Jessica dined alone. Having got rid of Aunt Eurice through the good offices of Grandmama, and having seen the other guests on their way a short time later, she had spent an uneventful day awaiting his arrival. It was not until around nine o'clock that she became troubled by doubts. She considered the folly of trusting her stepfather to keep his word when he had sought to have both her and her husband murdered; and this reflection put her in a fair way of thinking treachery might have befallen Acton. By shortly after ten she knew there was only one thing for it if she were to have peace of mind: she must go to London.

Rising at an early hour the following morning, she packed a valise and went downstairs. The porter seemed astonished to see her, but went off to execute her order to have Lottie brought around. When she had consumed a dish of bacon and eggs and had drunk two cups of coffee, she informed Saunders that the mare could be collected at the inn in the village, and rode off with the valise balanced somewhat precariously across her lap. Few people were to be seen in the streets so early in the morning and only two shops had removed their shutters, but at the inn the servants were bustling about the kitchen and were setting the rooms to rights. The coach was not due to leave for London until eight o'clock. Jessica, having booked a seat, and having charged the ostler with Lottie's care, went into the inn to pass the time before the stage was due to depart. One other passenger was fortifying himself for the journey ahead, but since Jessica had already had her breakfast she contented herself with coffee.

In the landlord's memory no member of the aristocracy, male or female, had ridden the common stage. The thought so appalled him that he ventured to explain to her Grace the evils, not to mention the discomforts (which he did, at length) of being jostled about for hours in the company of, in his words, "only heaven knew who." Jessica, thinking some explanation in order, informed him that she needed to go to London, that the estate vehicles were occupied in transporting departed guests, and that since her own curricle had been left in town (it shocked him further to learn that a lady should possess such a contrivance) she had no recourse but to make use of public transportation. With the deepest misgiving, he escorted her outside when the coach put in its appearance, and saw her take a place beside a farmer's wife with a baby clasped against her ample bosom, and facing the thin man whom he had previously judged to be an apprentice clerk. The steps were let up, and the landlord stepped back, shaking his head dolefully as the vehicle set forward on its ponderous journey to London.

By the time the coach had reached Stepson Green, Jessica was regretting the impulse that had put her in the swaying and rocking stage. Her teeth fairly rattled in her head at the jostling, and to make matters worse, the other passengers maintained a stoic silence, answering her few tentative remarks with startled glances and mumbled replies. The stop saw the departure of the thin man, and the addition of two further passengers, a couple on their way to visit a married daughter. The mother and her baby were set down two stops later, and a farmer and his son were taken up. For the next miles Jessica listened with what show of interest she could muster to the mother's account of evils that had overtaken her oldest-born. The daughter, it developed, had only recovered from the birth of her youngest when her eldest had had the misfortune to break his arm. Jessica sympathized with the daughter's plight, and clucked her tongue over the trials of rearing young as recounted by the farmer.

At the next stage, which was Northridge, a stout woman with a wicker hamper was taken up, and Jessica found herself squeezed in between this latest addition to their number and the farmer's son, who seemed to divide his time equally between gnawing at his nails and sniffling. No sooner had the coach resumed its lumbering progress than the stout woman opened the hamper on her knees, and brought forth fried chicken. Jessica, eyeing the gusto with which she chewed, felt slightly nauseous, and, leaning her head back against the faded squabs, closed her eyes.

In London, Acton descended the front steps of Acton House, pulling on his gloves. "Come along to

Aynesworth when you have seen Orling aboard ship,"
he said to Mr. Browning. "I'm sure he won't back out,
but I'll rest easier to know him out of the country."

The secretary answered in the affirmative and
watched him mount to his seat, with the groom up
beside him. "Stand away from their heads," Acton
commanded the stable boy. "They are in fine fettle,"
he remarked to the groom as the greys surged forward
around St. James's Square. He was obliged to hold
them to a sedate pace when they turned into Pall
Mall and on up St. James's Street to Picadilly. They
were not an easy team to handle and danced with
impatience at the slow progress through the crowded
streets, but once past the outskirts of the city he gave
them their heads on the stretch of highway to Cogham,
and the miles flashed past. By the time the phaeton
reached Bathern Regis, pale sunlight had begun at
last to break through the clouds. Acton stopped at the
best posting inn, ordered the greys rubbed down and
walked, and went into the inn. When he had partaken
of a luncheon consisting of cold meats and fruit, he
ordered the greys put to again, and drove on towards
Aynesworth at a spanking pace, arriving at his desti-
nation shortly after three o'clock.

Fifteen minutes later, having conducted an interview with Saunders which left him seething and the
butler flustered, he ordered the bays put to, curtly
dispensed with the grooms' services, and drove off
alone in the direction of the village. The intelligence
gleaned at the inn did nothing to cool his temper.
The stagecoach, the innkeeper informed him, could
not be many miles past Thornwood, it not being
likely to have made much better than eight miles an
hour. His Grace, he calculated, could easily catch up
with it before nightfall.

This proved accurate. The sun was just dropping below the horizon when the rear of the green-and-gold monstrosity appeared ahead, lurching and swaying top-heavily in the center of the road. Acton blew up a blast on the yard of tin, thundered past the stage, and drew his phaeton to a halt across the highway. The coachman, finding the road blocked, pulled up his team and sat glaring balefully as Acton jumped down from his seat, strode to the coach, and jerked open the door.

Jessica, releasing an involuntary gasp, found herself staring into a pair of blazing eyes. A softly uttered "Oh!" came from her lips.

"Madam!" he spat at her holding the door wide.

The other occupants of the coach had by this time recovered the use of their tongues and demanded in strident tones to know the reason for such godless goings-on up on the King's Highway. Jessica, under cover of the confusion, crawled across the feet of her neighbour and allowed Acton to hand her down. She wanted to explain, but one glance at his face decided her against it. She walked beside him as he stalked to the phaeton, where he helped her none too gently to her seat, took his own place, and signaled the bays to move forward.

The first miles were accomplished in silence. Acton's lips were clamped together in anger, and Jessica deemed it wise not to be the first to speak. The atmosphere was becoming very strained when he suddenly said curtly, "Perhaps you will be so good as to inform me what you had in mind when you embarked on this ill-advised journey."

"The more I think of it, the more I wonder about it myself," she said, stung. "It is hard indeed to have worried so about someone who doesn't deserve it."

"Ha!" he snorted in derision. "If I needed anything to enforce my belief that you are totally lacking in judgment, this latest escapade has supplied it."

"You need only add that I have precipitated a scandal, and your day will be complete."

"Don't be ridiculous," he said irritably, turning his head to glower at her. "I haven't the least doubt you know exactly what I mean. You may resent my interference, but you will conduct yourself in a manner befitting your position."

"Well, of all the unjust things to say! Next you will be telling me how I should act!"

"With dignity, Madam. With dignity."

"God grant me patience! You must think I have some very odd notions indeed."

"I know what your notions are. You thought to vex me."

"Vex you?" she echoed, astonished. "I was sure my stepfather had done you harm. You had not sent me word."

That drew his surprised gaze to her face. "It had not crossed my mind that I needed to. I have been away two days—three, if you count today. That's hardly enough time to cause you to worry."

"I suppose I was a bit hasty," she admitted candidly. "Remind me never again to book passage on the stage."

A smile played on his lips. "Quite done up, are you?" he said in moderated tones.

"Don't, I implore you, get me started on that. I would never get around to quizzing you on what happened in London."

He looked down at her, a thoughtful expression on his face. "Are you quite certain you wish to know? It could make you uncomfortable."

"I stopped allowing my stepfather to make me uncomfortable years ago. It was my only defense."

"You may console yourself with the knowledge that you need never again set eyes on him. I have succeeded in sending him out of the country."

"Oh, Acton," she breathed happily. "I'm so glad. Tell me about it."

"Make yourself comfortable," he invited, putting an arm about her shoulders. "He did his best to deny everything, but I confronted him with the testimony of his hireling, and he did finally break down. I was quite sure, you see, that he is basically weak, so it was really quite easy for me to dangle the possibility of arrest under his nose."

"Could you have offered proof to a grand jury?"

"Not really. It would have been the word of a criminal against that of an aristocrat, and I'm sure Orling's coachman would testify in his favour. Fortunately for us, he has never made a push to understand the first thing about the law."

"I still don't understand how you induced him to leave."

"I bought him off," he said bluntly. "He has been losing heavily at the tables. In fact, my dear, he gambled away everything."

"Good Lord," Jessica exclaimed, sitting erect. "I wouldn't for the world have you give him one farthing."

"Well, I've done it," he replied in his matter-of-fact way. "I wasn't foolish enough to hand over a substantial sum. He will receive an allowance which will continue for as long as he stays out of England. On the whole," he added, pulling her back against his side, "I believe we have come out of it fairly well."

"You might have told me," Jessica said.

"I might, but I knew you would object. You have not asked after the Inspector's progress in his investigation of McClean's murder," he added, chuckling. "Give me a kiss, and I will tell you."

"Now?" she exclaimed, startled. "The horses will bolt."

"Are you questioning my ability to control my team?" he asked in amusement, and forthwith demonstrated his equine talents most thoroughly.

"Have you quite finished?" she asked saucily upon emerging from his embrace.

"For the moment, sweet. For the moment. You put me out of mind of what I wished to say."

She looked at him, eyes dancing with laughter. "It concerned the Inspector."

"So it did, poor man. I thought he was going to burst into tears. The murders of Imogene and Froggie were McClean's first attempt to dispose of me. He thought it logical to assume I would be accused, found guilty, and hanged. Courtney claims to have remained silent through fear for his own life."

"Will he be punished? I should think he would."

"He will, but for more serious crimes. You may perhaps realize that while I remained single McClean felt no pressing need to be rid of me. By marrying you, I placed both our lives in jeopardy. The failure of the murders to put a noose around my neck made it necessary for McClean to act quickly before you bore me an heir of my own. Courtney provided him with a ruffian whom he hired to shoot us in our coach. Our deaths would thus appear the work of a highwayman."

She shook her head in disbelief. "It is too shocking to contemplate," she said after a moment. "My God! McClean must have been the worst sort of paperskulled gapeseed to think he could get away with it."

"He was insane, Jessica."

"I've been told that a madman can be quite clever at times."

"You will admit only a madman would hire a killer and then set forth himself in a marked coach. There could be only one outcome of such a foolish act. A sane man would have foreseen it."

"One must regret McClean. He had not the resolution to accept life as he found it; but it must have been hard indeed not to have been born to a station he could accept."

"Yes, of course it was. But you are entirely too tender-hearted, my dear. Other men, when faced with the same disappointment, would hardly resort to murder."

"I must own that you are right, though a spoiled life must always be held a pity. Tell me, Acton. How is any of this to be put to Courtney's account?"

"Meeks, who was McClean's butler, felt a jury might be very interested in his own part in the affair, and became most cooperative. His testimony will put Courtney away for years to come."

She bit her lip. "We have been made a pair of sitting ducks. I really had no idea that marriage could produce such shattering consequences."

"For myself, I make no apologies. You would have made any consideration of personal safety quite without merit. I am exceedingly sorry for any danger I brought on you."

"Oh," she said foolishly. "You, my love, made any of my own considerations quite unimportant."

He guided his team to the verge beside the road, and drew them to a halt. Hitching up his reins, he turned and swept her into his arms. "Acton," she gasped, emerging from the embrace. "It is most improper, kissing on a public highway."

"Fine words from a duchess who would ride the public stage," he murmured against her lips, and kissed her again.

"Dignity, Sir," she said, trying to suppress a laugh. "Dignity. That's the thing."

*The irresistible love story
with a happy ending.*

THE PROMISE

A novel by
DANIELLE STEEL

Based on a screenplay by
GARRY MICHAEL WHITE

After an automobile accident which left Nancy McAllister's
beautiful face a tragic ruin, she accepted the money for plastic
surgery from her lover's mother on one condition: that she never
contact Michael again. She didn't know Michael would be told
that she was dead.

Four years later, Michael met a lovely woman whose face he
didn't recognize, and wondered why she hated him with such
intensity . . .

A Dell Book $1.95

Dell's Delightful
Candlelight Romances

*A tumultuous drama
of misplaced love
and betrayal*

Scarlet Shadows

by Emma Drummond

Sweet, innocent, beautiful Victoria Castledon loved her dashing
and aristocratic husband, Charles Sanford. Or at least she thought
she did, until she met the notorious Captain Esterly. He alone
could awaken Victoria to the flaming desires within her, and she
would not be happy until she yielded to love's sweet torment . . .

From London to Constantinople Victoria pursues Captain Esterly
only to find out that this man she so desperately loves is her
husband's brother. Her scandalous desire blazed across continents
—setting brother against brother, husband against husband, lover
against lover . . .

A DELL BOOK $2.25

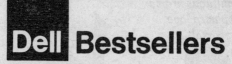

Dell Bestsellers